BLUEBONNET
SPRING

BLUEBONNET SPRING

•

Amanda Harte

AVALON BOOKS
NEW YORK

PRINTED IN THE UNITED STATES OF AMERICA
ON ACID-FREE PAPER
BY HADDON CRAFTSMEN, BLOOMSBURG, PENNSYLVANIA

For Patricia Villeneuve,
whose hospitality is as large
as the state of Texas and
whose friendship knows no bounds.

Chapter One

It was a mistake. A colossal mistake. Rebecca Barton settled back in the surprisingly comfortable rattan chair and tried to relax. She could tell herself that the problem was jet lag. After all, it had taken close to twelve hours of flying to get from Canela to Hilo. But Rebecca had never been one for self deception. She knew the problem wasn't jet lag, nor was it simple fatigue.

Think of something positive, she told herself. That was the advice the grief counselor had given her. *Find something good in every day*. It was sound advice, and on most days it worked. The problem was, today everything good in Rebecca's life was thousands of miles away. If she wanted to be happy, she should have stayed home.

Rebecca opened the menu and studied the choices. As befitted a five-star adults-only resort, each entrée sounded more delicious than the preceding one. And because this five-star resort was Hawaiian, the appetizers were an enticing combination of traditional tourist fare and island specialties. There was nothing wrong with the menu, and there was certainly nothing wrong with the restaurant. Three walls opened to the outside, providing spectacular views of the ocean, while soft trade breezes wafted the scents of exotic flowers through the dining room. The white linen tablecloths and heavy silver flatware gave the room a formal air that was only partially dispelled by the waiters' brightly colored shirts and the torches that cast long shadows on the floor. No matter how much she missed Danny and Laura, there was no denying that this was paradise, pure and simple.

As the pianist began a new song, Rebecca's lips curved in a wry smile. "Stranger in Paradise." How appropriate. This was paradise, and she was definitely a stranger here, a single woman in a place designed for couples. She shouldn't have come! The majority of the tables were for two—two newlyweds, their hands clasped on top of the tablecloth, their eyes shining with happiness, or two people celebrating a special anniversary, his island shirt matching her colorful muumuu, their happiness no less obvious than the newlyweds'.

Rebecca took a sip of water, trying to ease the lump that had settled in her throat. This was a mistake. Research was all fine and good, but she should never have come to the spot where she and Tim had planned to celebrate their silver anniversary. An elegant Hawaiian resort was not the place for a widow with two children and a brown dachshund waiting for her at home in Texas. Coming here was a mistake, a definite mistake.

Focus on the presentation, Rebecca told herself as the waiter moved the crystal pitcher of water to make room for a fresh fruit platter. Like everything else at the Bradford, the fruit was perfect. Instead of laying slices of mango, guava, and papaya haphazardly on the plate, the chef had cut each in the shape of a different tropical flower, carefully arranging them, then adding a stem of pineapple to create an edible bouquet. It was almost too beautiful to eat.

Resolutely Rebecca picked up her fork. The sooner she

ate, the sooner she could leave this assembly of happily married couples. At least when she was back in her room or even poolside, she wouldn't feel so conspicuously alone. Here, she was the only solitary diner, and it hurt. Instead of breaking through the lethargy that had plagued her since Tim's death, eating alone reminded her of how much her life had changed. Though the fruit was as delicious as it was beautiful, Rebecca wished she were back home at the local Sonic, watching Danny dip his fries in ketchup and giving little Laura a sip of her chocolate shake.

Focus on the presentation, Rebecca admonished herself again. This wasn't supposed to be a vacation; it was a learning experience. That was part of the argument Rachel had used when she had suggested Rebecca book the trip. "You'll see how the best resorts are run," her sister had said.

As if she heard Rachel's voice, Rebecca buttered a roll, noting that both the bread and the butter had been formed in the shape of a *B*. Though understated, the Bradford Resort did not hesitate to remind its guests where they were. When the family that had founded the famous Manhattan jewelry store had decided to expand its holdings, it had decreed that each portion of the Bradford empire would use the trademark initial that had long embellished jewelry boxes and shopping bags. Rebecca made a mental note to consider a fanciful logo if she opened her own . . .

Her train of thought derailed at the sight of the man approaching her table. While others strolled, their slower pace seemingly in sync with the resort's relaxed atmosphere, this man strode. That was unusual. Even more unusual was the angle of his head and shoulders, which seemed to announce that this was a man with a purpose. Though he wore resort clothing—a short-sleeved polo shirt and khaki pants—Rebecca could picture him in a custom-made suit, walking confidently to the head of a corporate boardroom.

She took a sip of water, trying not to stare. It was difficult, though, for this was a man unlike anyone in Canela, Texas. He was tall with dark brown hair, broad shoulders, and a face that could have graced a magazine cover. There were handsome men in Canela, but none with this level of polish and sophistication, and none who—despite his undeniable good looks—appeared to be in the wrong place. This man did not look like one who wanted to relax in Hawaii. Rebecca took a bite of papaya. In all likelihood, the man's wife had chosen the resort, and he had simply acquiesced.

As the maitre d' escorted the stranger to the table next to hers, Rebecca took a deep breath, looking for his wife. But the man was alone, a fact that the waiter's rapid removal of the second table setting confirmed. Her interest piqued, Rebecca wondered why a man like that was alone in a honeymoon paradise.

Spearing the last piece of pineapple, she stared at the ocean. In a few minutes, the sun would begin to set. Hawaiian sunsets, she had heard, were among the world's most spectacular. The couples would hold hands, oohing and ahing over the beauty, while Rebecca would . . . What would she do?

She darted a glance at the man next to her. As a teenager, a man as tall and handsome as this one would have made her nervous. She had never liked tall men, for their height made her feel shorter than her five feet three inches. And she definitely hadn't liked men whose perfect physiques reminded her that she was twenty pounds overweight. Tonight, however, the man's presence helped Rebecca relax. It wasn't simply that she had lost those extra pounds or that the short, casual hairstyle she had adopted after Laura's birth emphasized her heart-shaped face and made her look like a gamine rather than a female version of the Dough Boy. No, the reason she had begun to relax was that she was no longer the only single diner. She might be a stranger in paradise, but she wasn't the only one.

As the waiter whisked away her plate, Rebecca heard the unmistakable sound of a cell phone ringing. She looked around, wondering who would let reality intrude on paradise. The answer was seated at the next table. Mr. Drop Dead Gorgeous unfolded his phone. Rebecca tried not to stare, but the man was seated between her and the ocean. Only a diner with a truly perverse sense of humor would prefer the sight of the kitchen door to the South Pacific; she did not.

Though a gust of wind made the torches flicker, nothing hid the stranger's expression. He stared straight ahead, his attention clearly focused on the conversation. It was, Rebecca realized, a one-sided conversation. The man had said nothing beyond the initial greeting, but the grim line of his mouth revealed first his shock, then his anger. Snapping the phone closed, he jumped to his feet.

Afterward, she wasn't sure whether the wind had caused the torch to flare or whether it was the man's motion that had disturbed the flame. All she knew was that as he strode past it, his arm brushed the fire. A second later, his shirt was burning.

No! Rebecca gasped in horror at the sight of flames rising from the man's arm and the smell of scorched flesh. For an instant everyone in the restaurant seemed frozen with shock. Even the man stopped moving. *Move!* Rebecca's brain shrieked. *He needs help.* Grabbing her water pitcher, Rebecca ran toward the man and tossed the cool liquid onto his arm. There was a brief sizzle, then nothing. Thank God! She had had enough water to douse the fire. Now if only the man hadn't been burned too badly. Rebecca grabbed the stranger's hand. "Let me see," she said as she studied his arm, grateful for her first aid training. Though the contact with the flames had been brief, it had been long enough to cause a nasty burn. "This looks serious," she told the man. "You'd better have the resort's doctor look at it."

The waiter who had materialized at Rebecca's side nodded his concurrence, but the injured man ignored him. He glared at Rebecca as if she had caused the fire, his brown eyes flashing with what appeared to be anger rather than pain. "Leave me alone!" he said between clenched teeth.

"You really need someone to look at that burn," she persisted. Perhaps he was still in shock and didn't realize how serious the injury was. Danny had been like that the day he'd fallen out of the tree. But this was not a six year old. This was a grown man, and judging from his scowl, he did not appreciate Rebecca's concern.

"Look, lady." This time there was no doubt. His voice, though carefully modulated, seethed with anger. "I don't know who you are, but where I come from, people understand the words 'leave me alone.'" He shook off her hand and strode toward the entrance, his head held in the same confident pose that had first attracted Rebecca's attention.

Though several other diners had risen when they had seen the fire, once it was extinguished, they had returned to their tables. Only the waiter remained. "We don't get many like him," the waiter said, his tone sympathetic. "Thank goodness," he added quietly.

Though the man had been inexcusably rude, Rebecca felt a twinge of sympathy for him. "It looks like this trip was a mistake for him." Silently she finished the sentence. *Too.*

Doug West lathered his face, trying to ignore the circles under his eyes and the rumbling of his stomach. The first were mute evidence of a sleepless night; the latter a reminder that he had eaten nothing since he'd landed in Hilo. After he'd gotten Lisa's call, he hadn't felt much like eating. If truth were told, he hadn't felt much like doing anything. He'd walked along the beach for what had seemed like hours, only vaguely aware of the waves lapping at the shore as he tried to make sense of his life. Then, when exhaustion and jet lag had finally claimed him, he had slept for a few hours.

Now here he was, shaving his face on what appeared to be a perfect day in paradise. The sun was streaming through the slats in the lanai doors, and he could hear birds calling to each other. Doug imagined that if he inhaled deeply enough, he would smell the fragrance of whatever flowers were growing outside his room.

He rinsed his razor, then dried his face and looked outside. The Bradford Resort was everything the brochure had claimed, the setting almost improbably beautiful, the weather faultless. It was the perfect place and the perfect day for a wedding. Only now that wedding would not take place. Doug tugged a shirt over his head, wincing slightly when the short sleeves abraded his arm in a tangible reminder of what had happened yesterday.

It was odd. He supposed he should feel a sense of loss. After all, it wasn't every day that a man had his engagement broken so dramatically. Though it would be an exaggeration to say that his heart was broken along with his engagement, surely he should feel some pain, something more than the throbbing of the burn on his arm. Instead, all he felt was annoyance that he had flown so far for no good reason. It wasn't as though Doug had had any desire to see Hawaii; that had been Lisa's idea. "It'll be so romantic," she had told him. So romantic that she had decided not to come, not to marry him, and if her words last night were to be believed, never to see him again. So much for romance.

Doug walked into the dining room. Though he could do nothing about the lack of sleep, he could assuage his hunger pangs. This morning there were no linen tablecloths, and, thank goodness, no lit torches. Even this early, the sun provided adequate illumination, leaving no need for supplemental lighting. As the maitre d' led Doug to the table he had been given last night, he saw that the blond woman who had doused the fire was seated next to him. The Bradford, it appeared, assigned guests to the same spot for the length of their stay.

When the maitre d' had left, Doug rose and walked the few steps to the woman's table. Though he was certain she could have heard him if he'd simply leaned in her direction, she deserved more courtesy than that. "I wouldn't blame you if you refuse to speak to me," Doug said, reacting to the surprise that colored her face when he stood beside her table. She was prettier than he recalled, not that he had been in a mood to notice much of anything yesterday. He had remembered that she was blond, but he hadn't realized her eyes were so blue. "I want to apologize for last night. I'm not usually so rude." His rudeness was one of the few things he regretted about the previous evening.

The woman nodded solemnly, as if she understood, and he noticed that her face was heart-shaped, her lips surprisingly full. Doug found himself wondering how those lips would look if she smiled. "It seemed that you were having a bad night," she said.

"You could say that."

The blond paused for a moment, and he could see the indecision on her face. Unlike Lisa and his female colleagues, this woman seemed to feel no need to hide her emotions. He had seen her surprise, and now she was weighing a decision. When she spoke, her words surprised him. "Would you like to join me for breakfast?" The woman gestured toward the empty seat across from her.

It was a gracious invitation, one he had no intention of refusing. Doug had never enjoyed eating alone, and this morning his thoughts were especially poor companions. With a nod toward the waiter to set the place, Doug pulled out the empty chair. "I'm Doug West," he said.

"And I'm Rebecca Barton. My friends call me Becky."

Doug couldn't help it. He raised one eyebrow in surprise. "Do you mind if I call you Rebecca? You don't seem like a Becky to me." Beckies, at least in Doug's experience, were cute young things, not elegant women like this one. Though her hair was short and tousled and her shirt casual, she had an innate elegance that appealed to Doug.

She shrugged. "Suit yourself."

After the waiter had filled his water glass and taken his order, Doug placed his hands on the table and leaned forward. "I want to thank you for being my Florence Nightingale last night." Remembering that Rebecca's last name was Barton, he added, "Or maybe I should thank you for being my Clara Barton." Her quick thinking had saved him from a more serious burn. He had been dimly aware of that last night, but at the time he'd been so angry that he could think of nothing other than getting out of the restaurant before he exploded.

"How is your arm?"

Doug glanced at it. Though his sleeve covered most of the burn, a portion of reddened skin was visible. "It hurts a bit," he admitted, "but I'll live." *And*, he added to himself, *the scar will remind me not to repeat my mistakes*.

While he waited for the waiter to bring his food, Doug reached for a bagel and slathered it with cream cheese. The smell of Rebecca's breakfast was making his mouth water with anticipation. If he didn't eat soon, his stomach might decide to rumble again, embarrassing him almost as much as last night's display of poor manners had.

"How long are you staying here?" Rebecca asked. It was an innocent question. She had no way of knowing that it would raise specters he was trying to bury.

How long was he staying? Not long at all. As far as he could see, he had already been here too long. "I'm leaving today." Doug took a bite of the bagel, trying not to frown when he realized that the cream cheese was flavored with pineapple.

One of Rebecca's eyebrows rose, and for a second Doug was afraid she had misinterpreted his frown and thought it was directed at her. Before he could explain that pineapple was not his favorite fruit, she spoke. "I must have misunderstood." Her blue eyes clouded with confusion. "I thought you arrived yesterday like me."

Doug washed down the bagel with a sip of coffee. While he might not have enjoyed the fruit flavored cream cheese, the coffee was excellent. "I did, but I'm going back to Michigan this afternoon."

Rebecca's hand stilled in the midst of pouring syrup on her French toast. "Do you mind my saying that Hawaii is awfully far to come for a dinner you didn't even eat?"

Doug shrugged. "Why would I mind your stating the obvious? The fact is, I had planned to be here for a week." He hadn't intended to say anything more, but there was something open, friendly, and yes, understanding about her expression. Doug waited until the waiter had placed the plate of bacon and eggs in front of him before he said, "I was supposed to be getting married today."

Though he saw a flicker of surprise in her eyes, Rebecca said nothing. She was not a woman to pry, Doug realized. Perhaps that was why he continued. "Last night's phone call was from my fiancé. My ex-fiancé, to be more precise. She broke our engagement."

Rebecca's eyes clouded again. "I'm so sorry. No wonder you were upset." Her words were commonplace, but the look she gave Doug told him that she understood pain. What, he wondered, had caused that pain? He wouldn't ask. Like Rebecca, Doug would not pry, and yet he found himself speculating on the reason Rebecca Barton seemed so sympathetic. Had she too experienced a broken engagement? She wasn't wearing a ring, but that proved little. Even some happily married women wore no rings.

"I've been telling myself that this is better than an ugly divorce in a year or so," he said when he had swallowed a forkful of eggs.

"That's undoubtedly true," Rebecca agreed, "but it still hurts. No one likes rejection."

Doug couldn't imagine who would have rejected a beautiful woman like Rebecca. "So, tell me about yourself," he said, curious as to why a woman who looked like her and who appeared to be both kind and friendly would have what appeared to be firsthand knowledge of pain and rejection.

She poured herself a second cup of coffee, stirring the sugar for so long that Doug suspected she was composing her reply. "There's not much to tell," Rebecca said at length. "I needed a change of pace, and Hawaii was as different from a small town in Texas as any place on earth."

She had said *I*, not *we*. "Then you're here alone." Though there had been no sign of a husband or friend, it was possible that her traveling companion was ill and had missed both meals.

"Yes." The way she picked up her cup and sipped the

coffee told Doug this was a subject Rebecca did not want to pursue, and so he changed the subject and spent the rest of the meal asking her for her impressions of the resort, speculating on whether she would see whales, even commenting on the excellence of the Kona coffee. Though the conversation was ordinary, her responses were not. Doug found that Rebecca Barton had a quirky sense of humor that extended to herself. Unlike many people he knew, she wasn't afraid to laugh at her own foibles. It was, Doug realized as he returned to his room, one of the most pleasant meals he could remember.

With a quick glance at his watch, he began tossing items into his suitcase. The airport shuttle was leaving in fifteen minutes. That would give him plenty of time. He yanked open the top dresser drawer and grabbed a handful of shirts. When the drawers were empty, he spun the combination on the room safe. Though Lisa would never wear the diamond encrusted band, he wasn't foolish enough to leave it behind. Tucking it into his carry-on bag, Doug reached for the remaining item in the safe. He opened the heavy envelope and stared at the itinerary for what should have been his honeymoon.

As he started to stuff the envelope into his carry-on, Doug paused, considering. It was a crazy scheme. Totally ridiculous. For a man not given to impulses, this was the most absurdly impulsive idea he'd ever had.

And yet . . .

Rebecca stretched her legs out on the chaise longue and opened her book. When she had driven her to the airport, Rachel had handed her sister a bag of paperbacks, insisting that all of them were guaranteed to keep her interest. "You'll love *Golden Web*," she had insisted, pointing to a Regency-era romance with one of the prettiest covers Rebecca had ever seen. "Trust me." Rebecca had enjoyed the mystery she'd read on the long flight to Hawaii. Maybe this book would hold her attention too.

Adjusting her hat to block the sun, Rebecca started to read. Ten minutes later, though she had turned a number of pages, she realized that she had no idea what was happening in the story. Her eyes had read words; her mind refused to register their meaning. Instead of the dashing blond Regency hero with his rakish smile, she kept picturing dark-haired Doug West, who—no matter how often he smiled—had an aura of sadness about him.

Her finger marking her place, Rebecca looked around. Only a few people frequented the fresh water pool at this time of the day. The majority, it appeared, preferred the beach. That was one of the reasons she had decided to sit by the pool—she would be less likely to have to engage in idle conversation with other guests. Although, she had to admit she had enjoyed her conversation with Doug, all except for the part where he'd mentioned how thankful he was that the Bradford didn't allow children, or—as he called them—rug rats. It was an innocent comment. He had no way of knowing that his words would remind her of how much she missed her own rug rats.

Even though she and Doug had discussed nothing of major substance, their light bantering had been fun. Imagine telling her she didn't look like a Becky! The first few times Doug had addressed her as Rebecca, she had been tempted to look around for a woman with that name. She was Becky. That was what people called her and how she thought of herself. The last time anyone had called her Rebecca had been the day Officer Wilkins had stopped her for doing thirty-one in a twenty-five mile an hour zone. That was not one of her favorite experiences. Why would she want to be called by a name that conjured those memories? And yet, she had to admit that her life had changed so much in the last year that she felt like a different person. Maybe Doug West was right and she needed a new name to go with her new life, the life that she was going to build as soon as she returned to Texas.

Stop it! she admonished herself. *Stop thinking about Doug.* They had spent half an hour together, strangers passing in the night, or in this case, in the morning. By now he would be on his way to the airport. She would never see him again, so there was no reason to remember how sad his eyes had been and how she had wished she could have said something to banish that sorrow. *Stop it, Rebecca. You can't help everyone.* She opened the book again and began to read.

"Mind if I join you?"

Rebecca looked up, certain that she had conjured his image. But it was no illusion. Doug West stood next to her chaise. He was wearing the same shorts and shirt that he'd worn to breakfast, although he had added a hat in deference to the tropical sun.

"Are you all packed?"

Surely it was her imagination that he looked uncomfortable as he sat on the chair beside her. "Not exactly." For a long moment he stared so intently at the palm tree next to Rebecca that she wondered if he were counting the fronds. When at length his gaze met hers, she saw uncertainty reflected in his eyes. How odd. Though his sadness had been evident at breakfast, she had seen no hint of anything resembling uncertainty. Quite the contrary. His posture, his gait, his whole demeanor had exuded confidence.

"I'm not usually at a loss for words," Doug said slowly. "I've presented business plans to venture capitalists and I've met with hostile labor unions. None of that bothered me, but this morning I can't seem to find the right way to say this."

Gone was the light bantering that had characterized their breakfast. Rebecca had no idea what was disturbing Doug, but whatever it was, it appeared serious, and she found herself touched by this sign of his vulnerability.

"My grandmother used to say that the best approach was to start at the beginning and keep it simple," she offered. Though she knew it was not her job to solve everyone's problems, Rebecca felt a connection to Doug. Perhaps it was because she had come to his aid last night. Perhaps it was because she saw him as another stranger in paradise. Whatever the cause, she felt compelled to help him, even if it was only by repeating her grandmother's homilies.

Doug looked at her for a moment, as if considering her words. Then he nodded. "Well . . . you see . . ." He paused, and she watched him take a deep breath. Had it been anyone other than this supremely confident man, she would have said he was trying to calm his nerves. He swallowed again, and then the words came out in a torrent. "I cleared my calendar for a week. The honeymoon is all planned and paid for, and it seems like a shame to waste it."

"So you're going to stay, after all." Though she wasn't certain why Doug was telling her about his change of plans, Rebecca nodded.

A young couple, probably newlyweds, jumped into the pool and began to race toward the other end. Rebecca smiled, remembering how she and Tim had done the same thing on their honeymoon. Of course, they had honeymooned in an inexpensive motel near San Antonio, not in one of the premier Hawaiian resorts.

Apparently oblivious to the swimmers, Doug stared at the ground. "Maybe . . . if . . ." There was no doubt that the man who had faced labor unions and venture capitalists was having trouble talking to an ordinary Texas widow. At length Doug raised his eyes to meet hers. "A honeymoon is for two."

Bewildered by the conversation, Rebecca could do

nothing other than nod again. "That's true," she said, her mystification growing.

He stared at her so intently that she wondered if she had suddenly sprouted a second nose. What was he trying to say? Why was he looking at her that way? Had she been mistaken in thinking that he was a decent man caught in an awkward situation? Rebecca swung her legs to the ground and prepared to leave.

As she did, Doug cleared his throat and leaned forward. "What I wanted to ask you, Rebecca," he said softly, "was whether you'd share my honeymoon."

Chapter Two

Rebecca felt the blood drain from her face. What on earth was the man thinking? Share his honeymoon? Absolutely, positively not. She had felt sympathy for him, but what he was asking was well beyond compassion.

"I beg your pardon," she said, pleased that her voice sounded cool and that none of her dismay was reflected in her words. "I hardly know you." She stood, drawing herself up to her full five feet three inches as she assessed the exit routes, trying to decide which would be the quickest. She had obviously been wrong in her initial impression, for the man appeared to be slightly crazy.

He smiled, and what was even crazier than his proposition was the way that warm grin could make a woman's blood boil. Jet lag. She was definitely suffering from jet lag. That was the only reason she was reacting this way. Sensible Becky—correction, sensible Rebecca—Barton had never felt this giddy around a man.

"I think we know a lot about each other." Doug contradicted her with another smile. "I know that you're kind and beautiful and have a sense of humor. You know that I'm sometimes clumsy but not always as rude as I was last night. If that's not enough, we'd have a week to get to know each other better."

He was definitely crazy—and more than just a little— if he thought she'd agree to his scheme. "I'm sorry," Rebecca said, taking a step toward the main lodge. Where were all the other guests when you needed them? The couple in the pool were so intent on their laps that Rebecca doubted they'd hear her if she cried for help. "I don't know what made you think I'd be interested in an arrangement like that, but I assure you, I'm not."

She took another step. Doug matched his pace to hers. "I didn't mean to offend you," he said in a voice that sounded both innocent and perfectly sane. The breeze blew his hair onto his forehead, making him appear boyish. Appearances, Rebecca reminded herself, could be misleading. "I just figured that since we were both alone, we might enjoy doing things together," he continued.

Rebecca stopped short. Was it possible that she had misunderstood him? "Exactly what kind of things did you have in mind?" she asked as calmly as she could, while her mind whirled at the thought that she had misjudged Doug's motives.

He pulled a folded sheet of paper from his back pocket and opened it. "A trip to the crater, a sunset cruise, a luau," he read. As he extended the page toward her, Rebecca saw that it was a list of activities that someone—perhaps a tour guide—had assembled for him.

"Oh!" She should have realized that a man like Doug West would have nothing more than a friendly interest in her. Jet lag. It had to be jet lag that had caused her imag- ination to imbue his perfectly innocent suggestion with not so innocent undertones. Though she did not meet his gaze, Rebecca could feel Doug's eyes on her.

"Did you think . . . ?" He stopped, apparently not

wanting to finish the sentence and put words to her thoughts.

Slowly, Rebecca nodded. "Yes," she admitted, feeling more than a little foolish. For Heaven's sake, it wasn't as if she were a beautiful young starlet. She was a widow on the wrong side of thirty, and despite all the dieting, she still had more generous curves than a model. She wasn't the kind of woman who caused men to whistle when she walked by, and she certainly wasn't the kind of woman who inspired declarations of love from men like Doug.

He let out a low chuckle. Rebecca flinched. How dare he laugh? Her head jerked up, and she glared at him. As quickly as it had risen, her annoyance faded when she sensed that he was laughing at himself, not her. "What is it about you, Rebecca Barton? It seems that I spend half my time apologizing to you." Doug's brown eyes sparkled with mirth. "Let me start over. I'm sorry if I wasn't clear about my proposal the first time." He handed her the sheet of paper. "That's what I'm proposing," he said, gesturing toward the itinerary. "Would you like to share my honeymoon activities package? No strings attached."

Rebecca smiled, thinking of how her sister had started her married life with giant strings attached. How ironic that Doug was offering Rebecca a honeymoon with none.

It was probably a mistake. She ought to say no. But she had come to Hawaii to get out of what her sister described as a rut deeper than the Grand Canyon. Spending a week with Doug West certainly qualified as a path out of the rut. "Yes," Rebecca said, trying to imagine her sister's expression if she learned of Doug's proposition. This was something Daredevil Rachel would do. Cautious Rebecca would never agree to a scheme like this. "I'd like that." She grinned at Doug with a sense of anticipation that had been sadly absent for the last year. Maybe this trip wasn't a mistake, after all.

*   *   *

"It's hard to believe that we're on the same island," Rebecca said a couple hours later. At Doug's suggestion, they'd asked the resort to pack them a picnic lunch and had hired a rental car. For a while they had hugged the coast, enjoying the sight of the endless surf breaking on the sand, but then Doug had headed inland, stopping only when they reached Volcano National Park. Now they were walking through a landscape more desolate than any Rebecca had ever seen. "We could be on the moon," she told Doug as she looked for signs of life in the giant crater. Though the rest of the island was lush, with almost unbelievable greenery, here the ground was gray rock, punctuated by only a handful of hardy plants.

"The guidebook says few tourists are aware of Hawaii's volcanic origins."

"You and your guidebook!" He had slipped it into his backpack and pulled it out to quote from it occasionally. Rebecca, whose few vacations had consisted of trips to familiar resorts on the Gulf Coast where there was no question about what anyone would do, was amazed by a man who obviously thought a vacation was a learning experience. For her, it had always been recreation, pure and simple.

She took a closer look at her surroundings. Though Rebecca had seen news clips of volcanoes, the pictures of red hot lava erupting from the top of a mountain and flowing toward the ocean had not prepared her for this solid gray wasteland.

"Blame it on my mother," Doug said with another of the grins that lit his face and turned him from movie star handsome into truly spectacular. "She was always reading, so it must have been contagious. At any rate, I discovered that books were a good way to learn things."

"Such as?" As Rebecca picked her way over the uneven

terrain, she darted a look at her companion. For a man who had been jilted less than twenty-four hours earlier, Doug West was certainly doing a good imitation of a contented tourist. The angry burn on his arm appeared to be the sole reminder of last night's unpleasantness.

He shrugged. "When I took over the helm at Apex, I learned about supply chain management and lean manufacturing."

Rebecca shook her head. The man might as well have been speaking Greek. "I hate to sound ignorant," she admitted, "but I don't have a clue what you're talking about." There was something almost surreal about walking through a volcano's crater, listening to a handsome stranger discussing his business.

"It's probably just as well. Besides the fact that we're on vacation and Emily Post or whoever it is that dictates good manners wouldn't consider this an appropriate topic of conversation, there's another problem. Lisa says once I get started talking about the company, I don't know when to stop."

"Lisa?" The second the question was out of her mouth, Rebecca regretted it. Hadn't she resolved that she wouldn't pry into Doug's life? This was going to be a week of pleasant activities with no strings attached, and that included not discussing personal lives. Since it was obvious Doug had no great love for children, she wouldn't burden him with stories of Danny and Laura. In return, she wouldn't ask him about his broken engagement. They would have no past or future, only one week of the present.

"Lisa's my fiancé. Ex-fiancé, to be more precise."

Of course. "I'm sorry. I didn't mean to bring up unhappy memories."

Doug shrugged again and slid the guidebook into his pack. "It's not as bad as I thought it would be. Lisa was probably right when she said I cared more for the company than her."

That had to be an exaggeration, the words of an angry woman. Rebecca couldn't imagine any man caring more for a business than a person. Not even her brother-in-law Scott, who was more involved with his gas station than most people were with their business, would have ever put it before his wife. But if it eased Doug's mind to talk about his company rather than his ex-fiancé, Rebecca wouldn't stop him.

"So, tell me about the company."

The trail they were climbing grew steep and narrow. Though initially Doug had suggested Rebecca lead the way to set the pace, now he moved past her, clambering over a large boulder, then reached back to help her. She put her hand in his. It was the simplest of gestures. There was nothing romantic about it, he was only helping her climb. And yet when her fingers touched his, Rebecca was sure she saw sparks shoot between them. She hadn't, of course. That happened only in books. But there was no denying the shiver that traveled from her fingertips up her arm. It reminded her of the day she had touched a plug with wet hands. There had been the same electrical current, only this time the sensation was pleasant, not painful.

Doug, it appeared, had felt nothing, for when they were once more on level ground, he said calmly, "Apex manufactures car parts. Filters, to be exact. We do both OEM and aftermarket sales."

He sounded so enthusiastic that Rebecca had a momentary thought that Lisa might have been right. Perhaps the company was Doug's whole life. After all, how many other men would be talking about their companies at the same time that they pointed out ripples in the lava flow?

Rebecca grinned at Doug. "Your TLA threw me."

"TLA?"

"Three letter acronym. You know, like OEM. I don't know what that is."

Doug handed her a bottle of water from the pack. "Sorry. When I start talking shop, I forget that not everyone knows the jargon. OEM stands for original equipment manufacturer. In plain English, for my company, that's the Detroit car manufacturers. Aftermarket are the sales to car owners. We sell through all the auto parts stores and mass merchandisers like Wal-Mart."

Rebecca took a sip of water and looked at the man who stood at the crater's rim, gazing into the distance. Doug West was different from the men she knew. Though they would talk about their work, it was usually to grouse about something. Other than Scott, who truly loved his gas station, Rebecca knew no one else who considered work as anything other than a means to earn a living. For Doug, it appeared, work *was* his living.

"How did you get interested in auto filters?" It wasn't a subject Rebecca would have considered fascinating, but Doug appeared to think it was.

"I suppose you'd say it was by accident." He reached for her water bottle and stowed it in one of the pack's zippered compartments. "When I got out of college, I worked for a car company. In their finance department, of all places. It was interesting work, but I wanted a change. Someone I knew mentioned that Apex was hiring management trainees, so I applied for the job, intending to stay there no more than a year. By then I figured I'd know what I really wanted to be when I grew up. The joke was on me," Doug said with a deprecating smile. "It turned out that running Apex was what I wanted to do."

"And now you're CEO."

"Guilty as charged."

Rebecca would be CEO—not to mention chief cook,

bottle washer, and scullery maid—if she opened an inn. Today, for the first time since Tim died, that sounded like fun.

Doug pushed the button and opened the sunroof. Although the rental car was equipped with air conditioning, the Hawaiian climate was too beautiful to need artificial enhancement. Other than the occasional light rain that dried almost as soon as it hit the ground, the days were faultlessly sunny with trade winds keeping the heat from becoming oppressive. It was, quite simply, paradise. Even better, he was sharing that paradise with one of the most relaxing people he'd ever met. Not that Rebecca was likely to feel flattered by the description. Women, Doug suspected, would prefer to be called exciting. They had no way of knowing just how much he valued relaxation. Especially this week.

He leaned back in the seat, glancing over at Rebecca. She sat there, staring out the windshield, her face lighting when she saw something particularly beautiful. It was so refreshing, not feeling that he had to entertain her every minute of the day. She didn't seem to mind silence. Unlike some women Doug knew, Rebecca didn't try to fill every moment with chatter. She seemed content to bask in the beauty of the island.

Of course, she also added a lot to the island's beauty. Though she seemed totally oblivious to it, Rebecca Barton was a lovely woman. Her heart-shaped face would make any man look twice, and when those blue eyes sparkled with happiness, even the ocean paled in contrast. But Rebecca was more than pretty. She had what Doug's mother would call good bones. In Mrs. West's parlance, that meant that her beauty would not fade with age. Doug smiled, picturing Rebecca with white hair and wrinkles, a grandchild cradled on her lap. He would not tell her about that picture. Though she might tolerate silence, Doug doubted she'd like knowing that he could envision her as a senior citizen.

He flicked on the turn signal, watching Rebecca from the corner of his eyes. When she didn't know that he was looking, he'd see that hint of sorrow that never quite seemed to disappear. Though she had not alluded to whatever had caused it and Doug felt uncomfortable asking, he was intrigued. No doubt about it, Rebecca Barton was a woman with depths he'd only begun to explore. Her silences, her quiet dignity, and yes, that beautiful face made a man want to know more.

"Almost there," he said as they pulled into the parking lot. They would be walking through a small canyon today on their way to the falls. Doug wondered if there'd be an opportunity to take her hand again. Purely as an experiment, of course. It had been a casual gesture when he'd helped her over the boulder in the crater. He had extended his hand to her, never expecting that the simple touch of her fingers would set his hand to tingling as if he'd touched an open electrical current. Doug had touched dozens of women's hands. Hundreds, probably, when you added in all the handshakes. Never before, not even when he'd been courting Lisa, had he felt that spark of excitement.

Exciting, yet relaxing. Quiet, yet expressive. Rebecca Barton was an unusual woman. And he was honeymooning with her. Who would have dreamed that the week would turn out this way?

"I thought you might enjoy a change of scenery," Doug said as they descended the stairs toward the waterfalls.

Rebecca's laughter seemed more melodic than the water that bubbled over rocks on its journey to the falls. "It's amazing. Hawaii is such a small place, but there's so much variety."

"This is the Big Island," Doug pointed out.

She grinned. "Have you forgotten that I'm from Texas?"

"Where everything is big."

"Not quite everything," Rebecca said with a self-deprecating smile. "My grandmother could never explain why I didn't grow to Texas size."

"I think you're perfect." Though another man might have said the words simply to comfort her, Doug didn't believe in uttering empty compliments. He meant it. It was odd. He used to like tall, thin women. Lisa was tall and thin. But this week had convinced him that small and curvy was better.

"You're a smooth talker." Rebecca's voice held more than a note of mockery.

"I always tell the truth." When she seemed uncomfortable with the compliment, Doug changed the conversation. "So, tell me about growing up in Texas. I assume your grandmother lived nearby." She had mentioned the older woman on several occasions, and each time her face had worn a fond expression.

"My sister and I lived with her. Our parents died when we were young, so Grandma Laura took us in."

Doug wondered if her parents' death was the reason for Rebecca's air of sadness. Though that was possible, he suspected that whatever had caused the almost imperceptible darkening of her eyes was more recent. "That must have been hard for her."

Rebecca's response confirmed Doug's belief that she had accepted her parents' deaths years ago. "If you listen to my sister, living with our grandmother was hard on us. I was lucky, because I got along with Grandma better than Rachel did, so I didn't think it was bad."

Rebecca paused when they reached a landing. Leaning against the rail, she smiled, and Doug wasn't sure whether she was smiling at the view of the tumbling water or memories of her childhood. "Canela is a small town," she said with another smile. "Everyone knows everyone's business and helps out. It was almost like being raised by the whole town."

She was painting a picture as foreign to Doug as the volcano's crater. "My childhood wasn't anything like that. I grew up in a suburb of Detroit where the neighbors all minded their own business."

The sorrow that never seemed too far from Rebecca's eyes increased. "That sounds lonely."

"I never thought of it that way."

Rebecca turned to face him, her expression intent. "Do you have any siblings?"

"No." Lisa used to say that was part of his problem, that he'd never had to share, and so he didn't understand how to share his life with real, live human beings, not just bricks and steel. That might be true, but Doug didn't want to think about Lisa or his childhood. What he wanted was to learn more about this woman who was so different from his former fiancé.

"I don't mean to pry," he said, knowing he was doing exactly that, "but I'm surprised you're not married."

Rebecca's smile faded, and she gripped the railing, as if to steady herself. "I was married," she said shortly. "Tim died a year ago."

Doug could have kicked himself. "I'm sorry." For so many things. Her husband's untimely death. The sorrow that haunted Rebecca's eyes. His own stupidity in asking.

"Let's talk about something else."

They did. Doug pulled out his guidebook, knowing his reliance on it amused her, and began to read the description of the waterfalls. The awkward moment passed.

As they walked down the path, Rebecca pointed to the tall bushes growing along the side. "That looks like bamboo," she said.

"It is. The guidebook says . . ."

She started to laugh, turning her head to grin at him. For a second, neither of them moved. Surely he couldn't be the only one who was mesmerized by the sparkle in her eyes, by the sheer delight of sharing a joke with her. Rebecca smiled again, but this time her smile held a hint of self-consciousness. As if suddenly aware that they were supposed to be on their way to the falls, she took a step forward. Perhaps the path was wet with spray from the waterfalls. Perhaps she simply lost her balance. Doug wasn't certain. All he knew was that she slipped. With the reactions that had served him so well over the years, he reached out and grabbed her arm, preventing her from tumbling forward. And as he did, Doug knew he hadn't imagined what had happened in the crater. There were sparks whenever they touched. Definite sparks.

The week passed more quickly than any Doug could remember. By unspoken consent, he and Rebecca shared a table in the dining room. Each morning at breakfast they would plan their day. Sometimes they took the excursions the travel agent had assured him would be the highlights of his honeymoon. Other times they stayed at the resort, relaxing by the pool, frolicking in the surf or doing nothing more strenuous than walking through the beautifully landscaped grounds. As far as Doug was concerned, it didn't matter what they did. Simply being with Rebecca was enjoyable. Today, however, they were on one of the planned excursions, and today for the first time he had not told her where they were going.

"I know you're going to laugh," he said as they drove out of the Bradford's front gates, "but the guidebook says that today's destination is the most beautiful spot on the island." That was why he had been determined to show it to her.

When she smiled, it was a gentle smile. "I'm not

laughing at you, you know," she said in the soft Texas drawl that was so easy on a man's ears. "I'm just amazed at how different we are. You're so organized that you make me feel like a scatterbrain."

"Calling me organized is being nice. The truth is, I'm compulsive. You're teaching me to be spontaneous." That was one of the things that had made the week so memorable—he was beginning to learn that not every minute of every day had to be planned in advance.

"Spontaneity's one thing you can't learn from a book."

"Touché!" Doug tried to keep his eyes on the road. The way it twisted and turned, he ought to give it his full attention. But that was difficult when the prettiest woman in Hawaii was sitting so close to him. Today she was dressed in a short denim skirt and a red gingham sleeveless blouse. Though he was not a fashion guru, Doug knew that gingham was not considered sophisticated, and yet he could find no fault with the way it looked on Rebecca Barton.

"Close your eyes," he said when they were a mile from their destination.

She shook her head. "Can't do that. I get car sick if I'm not looking out the windows."

Doug would take his chances. "It's only a mile. Trust me." The words were casual, but as he heard himself saying them, he realized how much he wanted this woman to trust him. Apparently she did, for her eyelids fluttered down. It was all Doug could do to wrench his gaze from that sweet face.

"Okay," he said as the car rounded the last curve and he pulled to the side of the road. "You can look now."

Though the scene was spectacular, Doug preferred to watch Rebecca, and he found himself holding his breath as he waited for her reaction. As he had hoped, her eyes

lit with pleasure, and her lips curved into a smile as spectacular as the view. "Oh, Doug! Is it real?"

He could understand her question. Though he had visited many beaches in his life, this was the first time he had
seen black sand. It was one thing to read the guidebook
and know that the sand was formed from pulverized lava,
the result of a volcanic eruption. That was a fact. But the
impact of white surf breaking on a perfect crescent
shaped beach the color of granite was something no
guidebook could describe.

"This is the most beautiful place I've ever seen."

Doug flashed Rebecca a quick grin. "Then the guidebook was right."

She shook her head. "No, you were right."

What was right was the way it felt, walking barefoot on
that beautiful beach with her, laughing as she checked the
soles of her feet to see whether the sand had colored
them, then somehow finding her hand clasped in his as
they strolled along the shore. Her hand was small,
dwarfed by his; she was tiny, reaching only to his shoulder. It should have felt awkward, matching his steps to
hers. And yet nothing had ever felt so right.

Perhaps the week would never end.

Chapter Three

"I love you too, sweetie." Rebecca gripped the phone as a pang of homesickness swept through her at the sound of her son's voice. Though it had been only a day since she had called them, it felt like a lifetime since she had seen her children. She glanced around her room, admiring the understated furniture that did not detract from the view of the Pacific Ocean. This was without a doubt the most beautiful hotel she'd ever seen, and Hawaii was the most beautiful place she'd ever been. She was learning a lot about hotels and how they were run, information that would be invaluable if she opened her inn. If only she weren't so far from her children!

"Please put Aunt Rachel on the line," she said to Danny, after he'd finished telling her about his beloved dog's antics. When her sister began talking about the latest happenings in Canela, Rebecca interrupted, knowing otherwise she'd never get in a word. "Danny sounds fine. Has he given you any trouble?"

Rebecca heard the clink of Rachel's earrings against the phone as she shook her head. "He tries to pretend he doesn't miss you," she said. "He told me he had to be brave for Laura."

"That sounds like my son." Though he was only six, Danny had tried to be the man of the house ever since Tim's death. "How's Laura?" The baby was still too young to talk, so Rachel had held the phone to let Laura hear her mother's voice. Rebecca wasn't sure what her daughter thought, but from her perspective, a coo and gurgles were not the same as holding her baby and seeing Laura's sweet smile.

"She seems amazingly contented playing with Mary," Rachel said. "You won't believe it when you see them together, but it's like they're sisters rather than cousins." Rachel's daughter was only three months younger than Laura. At first Laura had ignored the other baby, but now it appeared she had accepted her cousin. Rebecca breathed a sigh of relief, knowing that the girls' becoming friends would make her sister's life easier this week.

Rachel's voice held a speculative tone as she said, "Tell me about you, sister dear. How do you like Hawaii?"

Rebecca couldn't help it. She grinned as she settled back into the comfortable chair. After years of scrimping and worrying about how she would pay the bills, it was still difficult to believe that she could afford such luxury. It was even more difficult to believe that she was actually considering what anyone would classify as a major lifestyle change. After all, she was the conservative sister, the one who had never left home.

"Hawaii is wonderful!" Rebecca said as she began to describe the places she had visited, carefully omitting all references to Doug. Though she loved her sister dearly and normally confided in her, Rebecca didn't want to provoke the teasing that would follow as surely as summer followed spring if she told Rachel about Doug. Now that she was happily married, Rachel had turned into an inveterate matchmaker. For the past six months, she had been urging Rebecca to begin dating, insisting that Danny and Laura needed a father as much as Rebecca needed a husband.

Though even Rachel would admit that Doug West was not a prospective husband, she would tease Rebecca mercilessly if she knew that she had spent the week with a handsome, single man. But, so long as she neglected to mention Doug, there was no reason not to tell Rachel how much she was enjoying her vacation. "I walked on the black sand beach at Kaimu today, and it was the most incredible experience!"

Rachel chuckled. "Why do I think it's not just a beach that has you so excited?"

Never a good liar, Rebecca was thankful that Rachel wasn't in the room with her. If she could see her face, she'd know how right she was.

"If you'd seen the beach," Rebecca said in a voice that was amazingly calm, "you'd know why I'm enthusiastic. It's magnificent!" And so was walking along that beach, hand in hand with Doug West.

"I'm not sure I believe you." Rachel always had been too perceptive. "But I'm glad you're happy. I guess you have to admit that your little sister knew what you needed."

Rebecca nodded. "Okay, Rachel. You won the bet. I'll buy you the biggest hot fudge sundae Canela has to offer." That was the least she owed her sister. "Listen up, little sis. This may be the only time in your life that you hear me say this, and I want you to enjoy it. You were right!"

"So, tell me, have you made any decisions about the inn?"

Rebecca shook her head, then realized her sister could not hear her gesture. "Not yet," she admitted. For years people had complimented Rebecca on her cooking and her hospitality, urging her to open a restaurant. Though the idea had intrigued her, opening a business was a risky—and expensive—proposition. A woman who could barely pay the bills couldn't seriously consider becoming an entrepreneur.

When Rebecca had received her inheritance from her grandmother, she and Tim had finally been able to pay off their bills and do something he had insisted was important—buy a large life insurance policy. "Just in case," Tim had said. "Just in case" had happened, and thanks to Tim's insurance policy, Rebecca Barton was now a wealthy widow. She could afford to take a few risks. She could afford to dream. And when she had allowed herself to dream, she had realized that what she wanted was not a restaurant but a country inn. She wanted to provide bed, breakfast, and dinner, not to mention an occasional box lunch, to her guests. That was one of the reasons she had come to the Bradford—to see how a five-star resort was run.

"But you're still thinking about it?" Rachel asked.

"Yes, and before you ask, yes, you were right in saying that the Bradford would give me some good ideas."

Rachel had also been right to insist that Rebecca pack an elegant evening gown. Though Rebecca had protested, convinced she would have no place to wear it, Rachel had calmly folded the shimmering royal blue silk and then stuffed tissue paper into the matching pumps. An hour later as she zipped the back of the dress and considered her reflection, Rebecca knew her sister had chosen well. The blue highlighted Rebecca's eyes while it complimented her fair skin and blond hair, and the deceptively simple lines flattered her newly sculpted figure. It was a beautiful dress, the perfect gown for what the travel agent had told Doug was the perfect finale to his honeymoon: a sunset dinner cruise.

When Doug knocked on the door of her cottage,

Rebecca took a deep breath. Though he had been handsome in his casual clothes, nothing had prepared her for the sight of him in a suit and tie. Dressed in normal business attire, he was more than handsome. He was magnificent.

"Hello," she said, suddenly shy. Why had she never realized just how tall he was and how imposing he could be? For a moment she was transported back to high school, hearing one of the boys call her Bulgy Becky. But the memory vanished as Doug smiled, the approving look in his eyes saying he would never taunt her.

He held out a florist's box. "I thought you might want to wear this."

Flowers. Rebecca swallowed. The last time anyone had given her flowers, it had been their fifth anniversary, and Tim had surprised her with a dozen red roses. At the time she had been so thrilled that she hadn't thought to wonder how he had paid for them when they were so deeply in debt. It was much later that Tim had admitted he had saved his lunch money for a month, going hungry so that he could buy her flowers.

Rebecca blinked the tears from her eyes as she opened the box. "Oh, Doug!" She gasped at the trio of orchids. Even here, they were an extravagant gift. She stared at the corsage for a second, then nodded as she made her decision. Wearing another man's flowers was not being disloyal to Tim. She would always love him; she would cherish the memory of their life together; she would delight in their son's resemblance to his father—but it was time that she built her own life. Her heart lighter than it had been in a year, Rebecca smiled. "Thank you, Doug. The orchids are beautiful."

He shrugged. "They're not as beautiful as you."

"Still the smooth talker," Rebecca said to cover her embarrassment. Only Tim had called her beautiful, and even then she had known he was seeing her through the eyes of love. But Doug didn't love her, and he'd told her he wasn't a flatterer. Was it possible that the woman who'd been the brunt of so much teasing as a teenager was beautiful?

Her skepticism must have shown, for Doug spoke again. "It's the simple truth," he insisted. "You're a beautiful woman, Rebecca."

She would accept his compliment as she had the flowers, as yet another item to be added to her memory book, saved for the proverbial rainy day when she returned to the real world. "And you're a handsome man."

Doug's chuckle warmed Rebecca almost as much as his compliments. "Then let's get this beautiful couple onto the boat."

The travel agent had not exaggerated. The dinner cruise was the perfect finale to a week in paradise. Though the boat could easily accommodate more, dinner had been limited to a dozen couples. As they sailed from the harbor, formally dressed waiters circulated on the deck, bringing trays of hors d'oeuvres and exotic beverages to the guests.

"The miniature quiches are particularly delicious, Madame," the waiter told Rebecca. Bemused that he assumed she and Doug were married, she reached for the tiny appetizer at the same time as Doug. When their fingers touched, it was like the afternoon in the volcano's crater: sparks seemed to leap between them. Afterward, Rebecca could not have said whether the quiche was as delicious as the waiter had claimed. All she knew was that Doug's touch had set her pulse to pounding.

Half an hour later the maitre d' seated them at one of the widely spaced tables. Rather than facing each other, as they did at the resort, they were placed next to each other so that they would both have a view of the ocean. Though it was a practical arrangement, Rebecca found it oddly disturbing to be so close to Doug. She sat next to him in the small rental car, but this was different. Here no console separated them, and when he moved his arm, she could feel a light breeze on her skin.

The scents of tropical flowers mingled with the mouth-watering aromas of their dinners, while the gentle lapping of the water formed a counterpoint to the pianist's medley of Broadway tunes. And while they ate, the sun continued its inexorable descent, turning the sky from red to orange to pink. By the time dessert and coffee were served, the sun had set and the sky was black. Rebecca felt a momentary pang that the sun was gone and their cruise was ending.

As if he sensed her thoughts, Doug pulled out her chair and led her to the back of the boat. "They promised us dancing."

"Dancing?"

Though the night was moonless, there was enough light for Rebecca to see the amused expression on his face. "What's the matter? Don't you think I know how to dance?"

She shook her head. "It wasn't you I was wondering about. I haven't danced in years. I'm not sure I remember how."

"It's supposed to be like riding a bicycle. You never forget."

"What if I told you that I was a less than Olympic caliber cyclist and that I failed dancing class?"

"I wouldn't believe you. But—just in case—let's have a pact. I won't complain if you step on my feet so long as you don't wince too much if I mangle your toes. Deal?"

"Deal."

As the music began and Doug drew her into his arms, Rebecca knew her fears were for naught. After the first few chords, their feet began to move as if they had done this hundreds of times, and before she knew what was happening, Rebecca realized that she was no longer worrying about the dance steps. Instead, she was concentrating on the music and how wonderful it felt to be gliding across the deck in the arms of the most handsome man she had ever met. They were dancing, but more than that, it felt as if she were floating, suspended in a moment of pure perfection.

The first song ended and the second began. As she recognized the tune, Rebecca's breath came out in a soft gasp.

"Something wrong?"

"No." She shook her head. "It's just that that's the song they were playing at dinner the first night right before you came in."

Doug listened for a moment. " 'Stranger in Paradise.' That's an oldie, isn't it?"

She nodded. "When I heard it that night, it seemed so appropriate. I was in paradise, and I certainly was a stranger."

"And now?"

"It's still paradise, but I don't feel like such a stranger any longer."

"I'm glad." And he said no more.

As they danced for another half hour, Rebecca was only vaguely aware that the boat had turned and that they were headed back toward the shore. When the final strains of "Good Night, Sweetheart" faded away and the other couples began to drift toward the railing, Doug led Rebecca toward the stern. Perhaps it was because the other guests were honeymooners and he didn't want her to feel out of place. Perhaps there was another reason why he held her hand as they walked. Rebecca didn't care. For the moment she felt safe and cherished. It was all an illusion that would disappear with the morning light, but for tonight she was going to revel in make-believe.

"Aren't the stars beautiful?" Doug leaned against the railing, his posture apparently casual, although the earnest expression she saw in his eyes gave lie to his nonchalance.

Poets had described them as diamonds sprinkled on a backdrop of black velvet. Others had claimed not even diamonds sparkled with the brilliance of the constellations. Rebecca didn't care. It was a perfect night, not because of the stars or the delicious food or the magnificent sunset. The night was perfect because she was with Doug.

She was never certain who turned or who made the first move. All she knew was that suddenly she was in Doug's arms, and his lips were on hers. It was a gentle kiss, as soft as a butterfly's wings. It lasted only a few seconds, and yet Rebecca knew she would never forget it. The perfect evening had a perfect ending.

"Orange juice is fine." Doug took the glass the flight attendant offered him, then settled back in the wide leather seat. In just a few minutes, the plane would take off, and he'd be on his way home. That was what he wanted, of course. He wanted to be back in Michigan, dealing with the sundry problems that constituted his business. Of course that was what he wanted. It was ridiculous to be thinking of a petite blond with a smile brighter than the tropical sun.

He pulled the airline magazine from the seat pocket and began to leaf through it. Surely there was something in it that would pique his interest. But, though he turned the pages, all Doug could picture were scenes from the last week. What a week it had been! He closed his eyes, remembering. It had started as a disaster, then quickly changed into one of the most enjoyable times of his entire life.

There should have been a hole in his heart, left by the fiancé who had jilted him at the last minute. There wasn't. He should have been desolate over his broken engagement.

He wasn't. Instead, Doug felt happier and more relaxed than he could remember. It was almost as if he were relieved that he wasn't marrying Lisa. That was absurd, of course. Just as it was absurd to keep thinking about Rebecca. And yet he couldn't stop. Rebecca was the reason the week had turned from disaster to delight. What a woman!

He wouldn't see her again. They both knew that they were two very different people with two very different lives. Each of them was realistic enough to know that their friendship was like a shipboard romance. It had flourished because of the setting. Once they were back in the real world, the week they had spent together would be no more than a pleasant memory. That was how it had to be.

Still, he owed her so much. The least he could do was acknowledge that in some way. Flowers. Women always liked flowers. Doug remembered the light in Rebecca's eyes when he had handed her the orchid corsage. Somehow she had kept it fresh and had pinned it on her sweater today. He could send her another one. Even better, he'd send her an orchid plant. That way she would have a lasting reminder of their week together.

But when he stepped off the plane in Detroit, Doug heard his name on the paging system. "Douglas West, dial zero on the white courtesy phone." At the same time, his cell phone began to ring.

"Thank goodness you're home," his assistant cried when she heard his voice. "We have a huge problem with Superior." All thoughts of Rebecca Barton and orchids were forgotten.

Eight hours and forty-seven minutes. Rebecca set her watch to Texas time and did the calculation. In less than nine hours, she'd be back in Canela. She would scoop Danny into her arms for a quick hug. As a six year old, she knew he wouldn't want to be held for too long, but surely he'd tolerate a hug. And then she'd cuddle Laura next to her heart. Her baby wouldn't mind if Mama held her a little too tight. How she had missed her children!

Rebecca twisted in the airplane seat, trying to find a comfortable position. It would be good to be home again, to see Danny and Laura, to resume her normal life. And yet she couldn't deny that Rachel had been right. Rebecca had needed the trip to Hawaii more than she had realized. The year since Tim's death had been a difficult one. Fortunately, thanks to his insurance policy, Rebecca had had no financial worries, but the strain of trying to build a new life and raise children as a single parent had taken its toll. She had been exhausted, both physically and emotionally. Now she was returning home a new woman, a woman with a purpose.

It had been a wonderful week. An unforgettable week. All because of Doug. Rebecca reclined her seat and stuffed a pillow behind her head. Closing her eyes, she pictured him. Tall, dark, and handsome might be a cliché, but some clichés were true. Doug West was tall, dark, and handsome, and Rebecca would never see him again. She knew that. She had no reason to go to Detroit, and there was certainly no inducement for Doug to come to Canela.

Rebecca touched the corsage he'd given her, reveling in the velvety feeling of the orchid's petals and remembered the surprise on Doug's face when he'd seen her wearing the flowers again today. The fact that theirs had been a passing friendship didn't diminish what they had shared.

It had been a wonderful experience. She and Doug had enjoyed a week of pleasurable activities. Though that was good, it was only part of what had made Rebecca's stay at the Bradford so extraordinary. The time she and Doug had spent together had shown her much more than the beauties of Hawaii. Being with him had shown her how other people lived.

Doug was a planner. She could laugh about his reliance on the guidebook, but watching the way he scheduled activities made Rebecca realize that she couldn't just keep drifting. For the past year, she had tried to live the same life she and Tim had shared. That hadn't worked. Without him, the life that had once been happy and satisfying was empty. Though she hadn't been ready to admit it, she had been trying to force herself into a role that was no longer the right one. No wonder she had been tired and frustrated.

Rebecca opened her eyes and stared at the ocean below her. It appeared as endless as the past year had felt. But that was over now. The indecision was gone. Starting immediately, she was going to take charge of her life. Doug had been right when he had said she didn't look like a Becky. Becky, the woman who had drifted for a year, was gone, replaced by Rebecca the Resolute.

Doug had been the catalyst, showing her that self-confidence and the desire to succeed were the necessary ingredients. Though she hadn't realized it a week ago, Rebecca now knew that she had those ingredients. She could do what Doug had done. She was strong and determined, and if she made mistakes, she would learn from them and become even stronger. There was no reason to continue dreaming, for she had everything she needed to turn her dream into reality.

She could do it. She *would* do it. Yes, indeed!

Chapter Four

One year later.

Rebecca leaned forward and pointed the remote at the TV. The children were asleep, the inn's few guests were in their rooms, and all the preparations for breakfast were complete. Barring an emergency, she was off duty for the next eight hours. Though normally she curled up with a book when she wanted to relax, tonight Rebecca was watching television . . . and it was all because of a book.

When she had heard that Lynette Thomas, the author of *Golden Web*, was going to be on Jonathan Stockton's show to discuss her new release, Rebecca had marked her calendar. *Golden Web*, one of the books that her sister had stuffed into Rebecca's flight bag for the trip to Hawaii, was the one Rebecca had started to read the morning that Doug had presented her with the preposterous proposition that she share his honeymoon. After that, there hadn't been time to read anything until the return flight.

Even before the plane had pushed away from the gate, Rebecca had been engrossed in the story and had not put the book down until she had finished it. Talk about page turners! The only disappointment had been discovering that the sequel wasn't out yet. Now it appeared the wait was over. Not only would Rebecca learn about Lynette Thomas' new book, but she'd also discover what the author was like. She could depend on the talk show host for that. Jonathan Stockton was noted for his unconventional but always entertaining interviews that revealed unexpected sides to celebrities.

As the show's credits began to roll, Rebecca leaned back in the rose velvet wing chair, propping her feet on the matching footstool. How she loved this room! Though the view was not as dramatic as from the inn's ten guest rooms, she had filled it with her favorite things—a comfortable chair with good lighting, a chair-side table big enough to hold a pitcher of iced tea, a tall bookcase already crammed with what Rebecca called her "keepers," and a canopied bed that one day might belong to Laura. Knowing that innkeeping could be hectic, Rebecca had designed the room as her refuge. Thankfully, thus far she had had few occasions to feel that she needed it for more than normal relaxation.

"Ladies and gentlemen." Rebecca adjusted the volume so that she would not miss a single word. "Let's welcome Lynette Thomas, or as she's now called, Judith Hibbard."

Rebecca felt her jaw drop in astonishment. She knew that name; she knew that face; she knew that woman! Judith Hibbard and her husband Glenn had spent a long weekend at Bluebonnet Spring the first month it was open. They'd been congenial guests, talking about any number of things, but not once had either of them mentioned that Judith was a bestselling author. Rebecca leaned forward, still trying to believe that she had had such a famous guest.

"The last time you joined us," Jonathan Stockton continued in the mellow voice that charmed millions of viewers, "you had a different name and a different appearance." The screen displayed two pictures, one of a redheaded woman with green eyes, the other picture of the woman Rebecca had met, a woman with brown hair and gray eyes behind oversized spectacles. "We now know that Lynette Thomas was a pseudonym and that the wig and colored contact lenses were part of a disguise. What made you decide to use your real name?"

The woman who had sat in Rebecca's dining room, nibbling pecan pralines and asking for a second carrot raisin muffin, laughed. "I found my real life hero," she told the audience.

Rebecca sighed, remembering how deeply in love Judith and Glenn had appeared to be. It was ridiculous to have these pangs of envy. She had had her chance at happiness. The years she and Tim had shared had been wonderful, if all too brief. Only a mean spirited woman would begrudge another couple the joy she had known. But that didn't keep Rebecca from wishing she and Tim had had more years together and that Danny and Laura still had a father to guide them on the journey to adulthood.

"Tell us about the book you've just started writing," Jonathan Stockton continued after his guest had regaled the audience with stories of how she had created *Silver Rose*, her new release. "I understand you're venturing from Regency England to wild west Texas. How on earth did that happen?"

Judith chuckled. "I didn't plan it, but as almost any author will tell you, sometimes inspiration comes when you least expect it." She leaned forward, giving Jonathan the warm smile that Rebecca had seen so often when the Hibbards had been her guests. "My husband and I were vacationing in Texas, and we found this absolutely marvelous country inn. The setting was so incredible that the minute I saw it, I could picture my hero and heroine there."

"Will you share this special hideaway with us?" Jonathan asked.

Rebecca held her breath. Could it be that Judith was talking about Bluebonnet Spring? Both she and Glenn had told Rebecca that they enjoyed the inn, and they'd taken dozens of pictures, but Rebecca knew that they had also planned to stay at two or three other inns before they returned to New Jersey. Perhaps one of those other inns was the one that had inspired Judith.

The author smiled again. "Of course. It's called Bluebonnet Spring, and it's in the Hill Country, not too far from Kerrville." Rebecca gasped, not quite believing that someone had just plugged her inn on national TV.

As soon as the segment was over, the phone rang. "Did you hear that?" her sister demanded without preamble.

"I can't believe it," Rebecca said, still reeling from the shock of discovering that one of her first guests was famous. "I have a copy of her book in the library, and she never said a thing about it."

"Rebecca, Rebecca, forget that. You know what this means for you and the inn, don't you? You're going to have a full house. Everybody in the world watches Stockton, and after hearing what Judith Hibbard said, they're all going to want to stay with you."

"I hope so." Rebecca crossed her fingers in the gesture she and Rachel had used as children. "I know the first six months are the worst, but I can't help but worry." Tim's insurance policy had made Bluebonnet Spring possible, but the money wouldn't last indefinitely. Within the next eighteen months, the inn needed to start making a profit or Rebecca would be forced to close it. She didn't want to even consider that possibility. Bluebonnet Spring was a dream come true; she couldn't let that dream turn into a nightmare.

When she had returned from Hawaii, refreshed by her

week away and inspired by Doug's example, Rebecca had decided to turn her dream of opening a country inn into reality. Though she had hoped to stay closer to Canela, none of the available locations had piqued her interest, and she had expanded her search, eventually reaching the Hill Country. When she'd found the old farm house and had seen the pond, Rebecca had known that nothing else would do. This was the place of her dreams, and—if she had anything to say about it—this was one dream that would come true.

The house had needed a lot of work—tearing down walls, installing bathrooms, gutting the kitchen—but it had all been worth it. It felt right. Though Rachel had teased Rebecca about instincts, insisting that business decisions should be based on facts, not emotions, Rebecca was not deterred. It was a fact, she told her sister, that she loved this spot. It was also a fact that her children were happy here, and that she herself was more content than she'd been since Tim's death.

There was something about this five-acre plot that filled her with the same peaceful feeling she'd had when she and Doug West had walked on the black sand beach at Kaimu. For a year, Rebecca had hugged those memories close, reminding herself of her week in paradise on days when the problems of reconstructing an old house seemed overwhelming. Hawaii was a moment out of time, never to be repeated, but the fact that the inn touched those same emotional chords confirmed that the move had been the right one.

"This could be the break I needed," she told her sister as her thoughts returned to the present. Judith Hibbard's unexpected endorsement might mean that the inn would finish its first year in the black.

When she hung up the phone, Rebecca pulled her copy of *Golden Web* from the bookcase. Then, impulsively she

48 *Amanda Harte*

went downstairs and retrieved the one she'd left in the guests' library. As she opened it to the title page, Rebecca's eyes widened. "Many thanks to the most gracious hostess in Texas," Judith Hibbard had written. "We'll be back!"

I hope so.

"You are one lucky man."

With a rueful look at the high tech equipment that was monitoring everything from his blood pressure to his brain waves, Doug wrinkled his nose. "Couldn't prove it by me." In his book, a lucky man was not spending time in the ICU. A truly lucky man would never see the inside of a hospital.

Still in surgical scrubs, Brad Windon frowned. "You knew the warning signs and did something about it. That makes you luckier than a lot of the men I see in here."

Lucky. There was that word again. "I can't take credit for knowing anything," Doug told the man who frequently played racquetball with him. "If I was lucky, it's because someone told me that nausea could be a precursor of a heart attack. I never knew that." When he had complained of indigestion hours after a meal, it had been one of his suppliers who had suggested a trip to the emergency room.

"Whatever." Brad shrugged and scribbled something on Doug's chart. "You're lucky you got here in time."

"Lucky too, that I had the best heart surgeon in Detroit." Doug wouldn't discount the role that Brad's skill had played in his survival. He had been fortunate that his friend was on duty when the ER had decided emergency surgery was needed.

"That too." Brad managed a grin. "Now make sure you don't undo all my fine work. I don't want you to go near that office of yours for a full month after we discharge you."

He was joking. Of course he was. Brad knew Doug and how integral he was to the daily operations of the company. After all, Brad had been one of the men who had predicted Doug would call the office at least once a day while he was honeymooning in Hawaii. Though Doug knew the surgeon couldn't be serious, Brad's expression looked as if he believed Apex could continue to run without him. "I'll work from home," Doug said when it was obvious that the doctor wouldn't release him without some sort of concession.

"That's not what I had in mind. You need complete rest, Doug, a change of pace. No stress." The doctor peered over the top of his reading glasses. "The best thing would be for you to go away somewhere where you'd have no worries. Find a place with no phone or television."

Doug was sure that Brad had never been to a place like that, or if he had, had spent no more than a weekend there. A whole month of being incommunicado was unthinkable. What on earth would he do, other than worry about Apex?

"I'm responsible for a company," Doug said, trying to keep his annoyance under control. If Brad saw spikes on the blood pressure chart, he was likely to extend the sentence. "I can't abandon Apex for a month."

But Brad wasn't backing down. "You weren't listening to me," he said sternly. "You have two choices. Either you turn the company over to someone so you can rest for a month, or you don't rest and then you turn it over to someone permanently. Do I have to spell it out any more clearly? I will if I need to." The lines between Brad's eyes reminded Doug of the evenings they had played racquetball when his friend had been unusually subdued. Those were

the days, Doug knew, when—despite Brad's skill—a
patient had died. "For Pete's sake, Doug," the surgeon
continued, "you're not just a patient. You're a friend. And
I want to beat you at racquetball in six months."

As he walked through the door, Brad turned. "If I were
you, I'd start thinking about someplace that specializes in
relaxation—maybe Bermuda or Hawaii."

It wouldn't be Hawaii, that's for sure. Though the week
he had spent there had been wonderful, Doug knew he
would never return. Some things, no matter how perfect,
were once in a lifetime experiences. Hawaii was one of
them. It wouldn't be the same, not without Rebecca and
not with him being treated like an invalid.

Though the tall brunette who entered the room a few
minutes later had a smile pasted on her face, she couldn't
hide her concern. "I saw the doc smiling," Terri Ashton
said as she stared at Doug, obviously trying to reassure
herself that her boss was still alive. "Must be good news."

"That depends on how you define 'good.'" Good was
like lucky. Everything was relative. "Brad wants me to go
away somewhere and rest for a month."

"Suppose he'd write me the same prescription?" One
of the things Doug had always liked about Terri and one
of the reasons he considered her his ideal administrative
assistant was that her finely honed sense of humor helped
defuse the gravity of daily life at Apex headquarters.
Today Doug wasn't certain he appreciated that sense of
humor.

"No need. I'll give you mine." Terri could laugh, but
being out of commission for a whole month was no laughing matter, not for a man like Doug.

His assistant pulled the visitor's chair closer to the bed.
"C'mon, boss. It won't be that bad," she said, her smile
firmly fixed in place, though her eyes couldn't disguise
her concern. "You might even like it better than Hawaii."

Hawaii. Why did everyone think he should go there? Hawaii was a place to honeymoon, not to recuperate from major surgery. When Doug shook his head, Terri continued, "I'll find a place where they have phones and electricity. You can take your laptop with you."

"What part of 'I won't go' don't you understand?" Terri was the best assistant he'd had. From the first week she'd worked for him, she'd anticipated his needs and had made his office run more smoothly than ever before. But today she was pushing the envelope.

Obviously ignoring him, Terri said, "I was watching TV the other night and I heard about this great country inn in Texas. It sounds perfect."

She wasn't listening. That much was clear. Doug frowned again. "If it's so perfect, you go."

As if he hadn't spoken, Terri continued, "I'll make the arrangements today."

"Now, sweetie, you know you like peas." Rebecca tried to coax a smile from her daughter. Normally Laura was not a fussy child, but today she'd flung her vegetables onto the floor, creating a sticky green mess.

Not for the first time, Rebecca was thankful that when she had renovated the kitchen she'd carved out enough space for a family dining area. Perhaps when they were older Danny and Laura could join the guests in the main dining room, but—as the pea-spattered floor demonstrated—that time was in the distant future. In the meantime, this corner of the kitchen was as childproof as Rebecca could make it. The polished hardwood floor was easy to clean, and she'd insisted on a high tech coating for the round country table so that it would resist scratches, dings, and spills.

"No!" As Laura shouted her favorite word, Rebecca closed her eyes for an instant, praying for strength to survive the terrible two's. Laura was still shy of that magic birthday, but she had already surpassed Danny's antics. Compared to his younger sister, Danny had been an angel. Was it, as Rachel claimed, simply the difference between girls and boys, or was it what Rebecca feared, the fact that Laura had no father in her life? The answer, Rebecca soon discovered, was neither.

"Laura doesn't like peas." Danny, who'd been sitting silently, devouring a huge helping of mashed potatoes, spoke up.

"Since when?" Rebecca had served peas earlier this week, and Laura had eaten hers without protest.

Danny's smile was guileless. "Since I told her she didn't."

Rebecca counted to three. She would never make it to ten before she exploded, and she knew it. "Oh, Danny," she said with a baleful look at her son, "you shouldn't have done that."

"But, Mom," the boy who looked so much like Tim protested, "peas are yucky."

"Ucky," Laura chimed in. Her adoring expression made it clear she'd do whatever her big brother said.

"What's yucky?"

Rebecca looked up from the mess she had been cleaning and smiled at the sandy-haired man who had just entered her kitchen. Jim Loeke had introduced himself and his landscaping service the first week that Rebecca moved to Bluebonnet Spring. His references had been impressive, his suggestions for the yard and garden even more so. Rebecca had hired him on the spot, and he'd been her friend as well as her landscaper ever since.

"So, what's yucky?" Jim repeated the question.

"Nothing," Rebecca replied at the same time that Danny said, "Peas."

"I see." Jim flashed the crooked smile that was one of

his most endearing features, then ruffled Laura's hair. "How are you, Squirt?" he asked the little girl in the high chair. When she grinned and reached a sticky hand toward him, Jim grabbed a paper towel and cleaned Laura's hands before he turned to Danny. "How's my boy?"

Though Danny had been smiling an instant before, he had no smiles for Jim. "I'm not your boy," he said, his expression sullen.

As Jim's lips thinned, Rebecca laid down the plate she'd been filling for Jim and faced her son. "Young man, I've had enough of your attitude tonight. Either you apologize to Jim, or you go to your room. Alone," she added firmly. "Doxy stays here." Danny considered being parted from his dachshund cruel and unusual punishment.

"Oh, Mom." Though spots of color rose to his cheeks, Rebecca noticed that Danny was careful not to look at their visitor. For the past two weeks, her normally gregarious son had been almost hostile to Jim, and she had no idea why.

"You heard me." Rebecca might not be able to force Danny to like her friend, but she most definitely could ensure that he was polite. From the moment that they'd learned she was pregnant, she and Tim had discussed how they would raise their children. Though they hadn't agreed on every detail, they'd both believed that good manners were essential. Even though Tim was no longer here to help her, Rebecca had no intention of raising small monsters.

Danny glared at her for a moment, then lowered his head. "Sorry, Jim," he said in a voice that sounded anything but repentant. And for the rest of the meal, he was uncharacteristically silent, making no comment when Jim suggested that the whole family accompany him on a picnic the next Sunday afternoon, even though picnics were normally one of Danny's favorite activities.

When the meal was over, Rebecca carried Laura up to bed, leaving Danny and his dog to play in the backyard. She returned to the kitchen half an hour later, expecting to see Jim reading the evening newspaper. Instead, she found him washing the last of the dishes.

"Oh, Jim, thanks!" He had cleared the table, loaded the dishwasher, and now he was scrubbing a casserole dish. "You didn't have to do that."

He shrugged. "It's the least I can do after a dinner like that. Besides, you know I want to help you . . . with a lot more than the dishes."

His expression was so earnest that Rebecca felt uncomfortable. Lately Jim had begun alluding to a shared future. Though Rebecca considered him a good friend, she wasn't certain she was ready for anything more than friendship. Jim, it appeared, had other ideas.

"I got some good news today," she said, deliberately changing the subject. "We're going to have a guest for a whole month, and he's taking Indian Paintbrush," she said, referring to the inn's largest room. Rather than number the rooms, she had given each of them the name of a native flower and had stenciled the flowers on the doors.

Water whooshed as Jim drained the sink. "A month. Any idea why he's staying so long? I didn't think singles stayed more than a few days." Rebecca had quoted Jim all the statistics, and they both knew that long stays were normally the purview of retired couples and families during the summer holidays. It was, as Jim had said, unusual to have a single person reserve a room for an extended period.

"Kate took the message. Something about recuperating from a heart attack." Rebecca tried not to shudder at the memories that those words evoked. "I'm not sure that's the real story. You know how Kate sometimes garbles things. She didn't even get the man's last name." Kate's errors were part of the reason Rebecca preferred to handle reservations herself.

"Kate was probably so excited that she forgot to ask all the questions."

"It's not just Kate. I'm excited too." Rebecca stood with her back to the window, admiring the cabinets that she'd ordered against her kitchen designer's recommendation. Though the style was simple, the blue milk paint finish had shocked the designer. "It's almost the same shade as bluebonnets," she had told him. "The cabinets will be perfect." And they were. When guests peeked into the kitchen, they invariably commented on the color scheme.

"The weekends are starting to fill up," Rebecca told Jim, "but even with the publicity on 'The Stockton Show,' we're still not as full as I'd like."

Jim took a step closer, his boots clacking on the floor. "It'll happen. You just need to be patient."

"Patience isn't my best trait." Rebecca had been in her element when she was renovating Bluebonnet Spring, because everything moved quickly. The first few months the inn had been open had also passed swiftly as she'd worked out the kinks. But then the waiting had begun— waiting for guests and waiting for the occupancy rate to reach the critical threshold.

More than once Jim had joked with her about her impatience. He wasn't joking now. He took another step closer, slipped his arm around Rebecca's waist and drew her to his side. "Then it's lucky I have enough for both of us."

Later that night while Danny was reading a story to her, Rebecca's mind began to wander. She had heard "Jack and the Beanstalk" so many times that she could practically recite it verbatim. Instead of listening to the familiar words, she studied her son's profile, marveling at the way his features combined Tim's dark hair with her nose and chin. In so many ways, Danny was a replica of his father. He looked like Tim had at the same age and he had Tim's sunny disposition. Most days. But there were days when he was undeniably moody, and those were the days that worried Rebecca. She didn't know what to do with him then.

Tim would have.

Rebecca's heart contracted at the thought of her son growing up without a father. He needed one, perhaps even more than Laura did. Laura had Danny as a role model and a masculine influence. Danny had no one. When they had lived in Canela, Rachel had assured Rebecca that her husband Scott would be a father figure for Danny, but now that they were several hours away, there was no one to fill that role on a regular basis. Danny needed a male influence. Rebecca knew that, just as she knew that Jim would be a good one. He was a kind man, a patient man, a man who enjoyed children. Rebecca knew all that.

Why, then, was she so hesitant to even consider the thought of marrying Jim?

Chapter Five

The Hill Country certainly was pretty. Doug grinned at the yellow sign. This section of the road had so many cautions that he'd started to clock the distance between them. Less than half a mile this time. It was about the hundredth warning of a narrow bridge, and there'd been at least that many yellow diamonds showing a corkscrew shaped road. For a man who'd had a love affair with the automobile since he was old enough to dream about driving and who actively searched out challenging highways, this was pure heaven. A driver's road if he'd ever seen one.

A driver's road. Hmmm. As he rounded the next bend, Doug slowed the car, considering. He and the rest of the Apex management team had agreed that they needed a new slogan, something that would be the foundation for a whole new advertising campaign. With the instincts that had served him well over the years, Doug knew he'd found the concept. His advertising mavens would polish it, agonizing over the precise sequence of syllables that would both intrigue consumers and be easily remembered. They'd argue and tweak and test market. That was their job. All Doug knew was that the phrase "driver's road" would be part of the new Apex slogan.

He tapped his fingers on the steering wheel and grinned. The adrenaline that was coursing through his veins owed little to the beautiful scenery. Though one part of his mind was registering his surroundings, the other began to imagine print ads and television commercials. They could show a driver in a car—different drivers, different cars, different roads. In each case, the driver would be laughing from sheer joy. The focus would be on the road, on the thrill of driving. Only at the end would they show the Apex logo and one of the filters. Brilliant! Doug made a mental note to thank Terri for sending him on this particular route.

He hadn't wanted to come. Relaxing wasn't something that came easily to Doug West. Why sugarcoat the truth? Relaxing wasn't something he knew how to do. It was a congenital impossibility. Hadn't he proven that in Hawaii? If he hadn't been engrossed in entertaining Rebecca Barton, in watching her delight at the sight of the Big Island's natural wonders, Doug would have gone stir crazy. That had been a week; this was a whole month. Until ten minutes ago, Doug couldn't imagine how he'd survive his enforced rest.

But Brad and Terri hadn't given him a choice, and so here he was, in the famed Texas Hill Country. Doug hadn't known what to expect. Hills, of course. Why else would they call it the Hill Country? But he hadn't realized there'd be fields covered with prickly pear cactus, herds of deer, the occasional goat farm, and almost as many trees as he'd seen in Michigan's Upper Peninsula. This was downright pretty. Good for business too.

Terri had booked the flight to San Antonio, then sent him up the interstate to Kerrville. At seventy-five miles an hour, Doug hadn't paid a lot of attention to the scenery. All that had changed the minute he'd found himself on a twisting back road. Terri was a genius, ordering a small nimble car and a convertible, to boot. The woman deserved a promotion or at least a bonus. Of course, he wouldn't tell her that he'd spent the drive planning Apex's next advertising campaign. Terri wouldn't consider that relaxation, and she'd probably report the infraction to Brad, who would try to do something drastic, like cut off Doug's cell phone. That wasn't going to happen. He was going to keep the cell phone and the laptop, and even if he was a thousand miles from the office, by the time the month was over, Apex would have its new advertising campaign.

Doug looked down at the odometer. According to the directions, he was only a couple miles from Bluebonnet Spring. He sighed, hoping the place wasn't as cute as it sounded. Cute wasn't something he could deal with, particularly not for a month. The name conjured images of individual cabins so heavily laden with gingerbread that they belonged in one of Grimm's fairy tales. One of the darker ones, that is. Of course they'd be painted blue. They'd probably be decorated with window boxes filled with—what else?—blue plastic flowers. Doug gritted his teeth. Just another mile. It would be around the next curve on the left side of the road.

As he rounded the bend, Doug took a deep breath and braced himself, then exhaled slowly when he saw the discreet sign and what would be his home for the next month. It wasn't cute. Not at all. It was beautiful and stately, and somehow it reminded him of the black sand beach at Kaimu. That was ridiculous, of course. This was the Texas Hill Country, not the Big Island of Hawaii. Nothing here looked at all like that crescent of volcanic sand with the milk white waves breaking on it, and there wasn't a palm tree in sight. The only thing the two locations had in common was beauty.

Bluebonnet Spring, despite its all too clever name, was a rambling farm house, two stories high, with a wide wraparound porch and one of the metal roofs that were so common in this part of the country. A number of ancient trees—live oaks or pecans, Doug wasn't sure which— shaded the house, while a meadow led to a small pond. Was this, he wondered, the spring that gave the inn its name? When he had first heard it, he had thought the reference was to the season when bluebonnets bloomed.

Without bothering to put up the car's top, Doug grabbed his laptop case, climbed the steps to the front door, and rang the bell, suddenly anxious to see the inside of the place that was to be his temporary home. First the idea for an ad campaign and now this surprisingly attractive inn. The trip was turning out better than he'd expected.

The door opened and a woman beckoned him to enter. "Welcome to Bluebonnet Spring."

It couldn't be. It was only because he'd been thinking about Hawaii that the woman's voice sounded familiar. Doug blinked, willing his eyes to adjust to the interior darkness. "Rebecca?" He tugged off his sunglasses and stared. Though it seemed impossible, this woman looked like the one who had shared his honeymoon. She was petite, blond, and had the heart-shaped face he remembered so well.

"Doug?" Her voice reflected the same uncertainty and disbelief that he'd heard in his own. "What are you doing here?"

There was no doubt about it. The woman who was welcoming him to the inn was the one he'd thought of so often for the past year. She was even wearing the same perfume that he'd found so alluring in Hawaii.

"I could ask you the same question," he retorted, trying to regain his equilibrium. What other surprises did today have in store for him? "I'm checking in for what is supposed to be a month's stay at the inn."

"You're Douglas."

She sounded shocked. Doug doubted she'd appreciate hearing that her face had turned as pale as her V-necked T-shirt or that he found her brightly colored toenails an incongruous combination with her denim skirt. "Sure was the last time I looked at my driver's license."

Rebecca Barton's laugh was as melodic as he'd remembered. "No wonder Kate didn't get your last name. Your secretary must have said 'Doug West,' and Kate heard 'Douglas.' She's a little scatterbrained, but she's good with guests, so I didn't make a big deal about the missing name." Rebecca gestured to Doug to come farther inside, then closed the door behind him. "I never guessed it was you."

The interior of the inn was as attractive as its exterior, furnished with an eclectic mixture of country farmhouse and English manor pieces that should have clashed, but instead intrigued Doug and made him want to explore the rest of the building. His gaze returned to Rebecca and he wondered what coincidence had put them in the same hotel a second time. This time, though, it appeared she was not a guest.

"What are you doing at Bluebonnet Spring?" Though she hadn't said much about her life in Texas, Doug hadn't pictured her working. He had gotten the impression that she was the stay-at-home wife type.

"I own it." They were three little words, but there was no ignoring the satisfaction in Rebecca's voice.

Doug hoped his face didn't reflect his surprise. How could he have been so wrong? All the time he'd talked about Apex and how he'd rebuilt the company, he'd never guessed she was also an entrepreneur. "I had no idea this was yours. You never mentioned it in Hawaii."

Rebecca shrugged. "It was nothing more than a dream then. It was only on the flight home that I decided to take a chance and turn that dream into reality."

Before Doug could reply, a man strode into the hallway. He was perhaps two inches shorter than Doug, with sandy hair and a tan that said he spent most of his days outside. "Honey, I picked up the mail when I was in town." When he saw Doug, the man stopped. "Oh, sorry."

The smile Rebecca gave him was as warm as the Texas sun. "Thanks, Jim." The tone of her voice told Doug that Jim was no casual visitor. "This is Doug West," she said, introducing the men. "He'll be staying with us for a month. Doug, this is Jim Locke."

Doug gave the other man an appraising look. It was evident from the way his eyes followed Rebecca that Jim Locke's feelings for her were far from casual. Was he Rebecca's husband? So what if he was? Doug tried to ignore the odd feeling that had settled in his stomach. It had been a year since he had seen Rebecca, and she had been widowed a year before that. Many women remarried within two years, especially beautiful young women like Rebecca. "Good to meet you, Jim," Doug said, pleased that his voice reflected none of the dismay that he was feeling. "Quite a place you've got here."

The man laid a possessive hand on Rebecca's shoulder. "It's all Rebecca's doing. I just help her out." Jim nodded, then left Doug and Rebecca alone.

Doug refused to frown. Of course she'd remarry. Rebecca was a woman with so much to offer a man, that it was a wonder she had still been single when Doug had met her. He swallowed, trying to dislodge the lump in his throat. It was totally ridiculous to feel as if he'd somehow been cheated. It wasn't as if he would have married her. He wasn't a marrying man. Lisa had shown him the fallacy of that particular life plan.

"Let me take you to your room." Rebecca broke the awkward silence and reached for Doug's laptop case.

"I can do that." He grabbed it back from her. It was bad enough that she'd married that blond cowboy; he wasn't going to let her treat him like a member of the geriatric set. "For Pete's sake, I'm not an invalid."

Rebecca's blue eyes filled with something that might have been anger but looked almost like fear. That was, of course, absurd. She had no reason to fear him. "You are here to rest," she said softly as she led him to the back of the house and the stairway.

Though she probably would have denied it, Doug was certain that Rebecca was climbing the stairs more slowly than normal, in deference to his health or lack thereof. It was a maddening thought that he was considered so frail that he couldn't run up the stairs two at a time. The truth was, he couldn't, and he didn't like that one bit.

"As you probably remember, resting isn't easy for me, but," he said as he looked at the staircase with its polished oak banister, "this is a beautiful place. If I can rest anywhere, it'll be here."

Rebecca's eyes sparkled, and this time there was no doubt that it was with pleasure. "I loved it the instant I saw it. This may sound strange, Doug, but it reminded me of Hawaii and the black sand beach."

One of the things he hadn't forgotten about that magical week in Hawaii was the way he and Rebecca had seemed to be on the same wavelength. Once he was back in Detroit, he had told himself that it hadn't really happened and that his memory was distorting reality. It appeared that his memory hadn't been faulty.

"That doesn't sound strange to me. I felt the same way when I rounded that last bend."

"The house was a wreck." Rebecca led the way down a long corridor. An Oriental runner softened the sound of footsteps but was narrow enough to show off the beautifully polished wood floor. Crystal sconces provided light, while a few reproductions of famous artworks added visual interest to the walls.

"I would never have guessed. You've worked wonders." Though her words told Doug that the inn had been reno- vated within the last year, it had none of the "too new" feeling that accompanied many renovations. This one had been done with forethought and taste, neither of which was surprising, given Rebecca's character. And Jim. Doug mustn't forget the man who was obviously an important part of the inn.

Rebecca opened the door to the last room. "You have a view of the back," she told him. "This is our largest room and the one I normally give to long-stay guests, but if you'd rather look out the front, I can switch you."

Doug shook his head. A quick glance told him that the room had a separate sitting area with a fireplace and a small desk that would be ideal for his work. Though he doubted there was much traffic, a room on the back side of the building would be quieter than one overlooking the circular driveway and the road.

As she showed him the bathroom, checking that there was an adequate supply of towels and soap, Rebecca explained the meal schedule. "Breakfast is so large that most guests don't feel they need lunch, so we don't serve lunch, but I can always arrange a box meal for you, or— if you're really brave—you can eat in the kitchen with the staff."

A staff that included her husband. No, thanks. As she left him to unpack, Doug tried not to frown. Fate had a strange sense of humor. A year ago it had put Rebecca in his path at exactly the right time. She had saved his arm from serious injury and—even more importantly—had turned his week in Hawaii from a disaster into one of the most enjoyable experiences of his life. Doug emptied the last of his clothes into a dresser drawer. Why quibble about it? That week in Hawaii was the single most enjoyable experience of his life. Now Fate had thrown them together again. Once again Doug's life was at a crossroads. But this time Rebecca couldn't rescue him, for this time she was married.

Doug stashed his suitcase in the closet. He wouldn't think about Rebecca's marriage. After all, he couldn't change it, and if there was one lesson he had learned early, it was not to dwell on things that couldn't be changed. He would work on something that could be changed: his ad campaign.

Doug picked up his phone and dialed Detroit.

"Danny, I need you to watch your sister for a minute." Rebecca smiled as her son put on his most serious expression and moved his chair an inch closer to Laura. There were so few guests tonight—only two in addition to Doug—that Rebecca was serving as both the wait staff and chef. This early in the inn's existence, she couldn't afford the extra cost of a waitress unless there were at least a dozen guests.

She grabbed the large tray and headed for the dining room, giving her children a final glance. As she did, she heard the distinctive sound of a cell phone turning on. Without even looking, she knew that the phone belonged to Doug.

"What happened to the Superior order?" Though he smiled as she cleared his salad plate, Rebecca knew that Doug's attention was focused on the person on the other end of the line. Some things, it appeared, never changed. The man might not have been born a workaholic, but it was a lesson he'd learned well. Rebecca had given him one of her three tables next to the window, thinking he would enjoy the view of the formal gardens. Instead, he was working. For all the attention he was paying to them, the gardens might as well have been paved.

Doug might not be looking at her beautifully land-scaped grounds, but Rebecca could not avoid looking at him. Nor did she want to avoid it. The man was as hand-some as ever. He'd changed into a cream colored golf shirt that highlighted his dark hair, and his loafers were slightly scuffed. On the surface, Doug West was the epit-ome of a relaxed vacationer, or he would be if he weren't talking on the phone and scribbling notes on a pad that had mysteriously appeared by his side.

"I hope you'll enjoy the stroganoff." Rebecca addressed the middle-aged couple who were her other guests. "It's one of our specialties." What she wasn't planning to tell them was that she had modified her normal recipe to make it "heart healthy." When she had learned that her long-stay guest was recuperating from a heart attack, Rebecca had searched for ways to lower the fat and cholesterol in her meals without reducing the flavor. It was amazing what yogurt and tofu could do!

Ten minutes later, she returned to the dining room. Although the couple were still eating, Doug had cleaned his plate. The phone and pad had disappeared.

"I thought the food at the Bradford was good," Doug said as Rebecca reached for his dishes, "but yours is better."

It was a simple compliment, far from the first she had received. Rebecca wanted her guests to enjoy the meals at Bluebonnet Spring. Doug was a guest who was enjoying dinner. That was what she wanted. Why, then, did his words make her feel as if she'd just been awarded the Nobel Prize for Innkeeping? Other guests' compliments did not have the same effect.

"Thank you," she said as calmly as she could. She would soon be over this crazy reaction. But when Rebecca returned to the dining room to refill her guests' iced tea glasses, Doug's fingers brushed hers. She should have been prepared. After all, the same thing had happened when he had touched her hand on that trail in Hawaii. But that had been a year ago, a lifetime ago. Rebecca hadn't expected the magnetism to have lasted.

Somehow she filled his glass without dropping either it or the pitcher. Somehow she carried on a normal conversation with the other guests. Somehow she managed to serve dessert and coffee without touching Doug's fingers again. But now that she was back in the kitchen, stacking plates in the dishwasher, she couldn't deny the fact that her hands were trembling.

This wasn't supposed to happen! When she had returned from Hawaii, Rebecca had tried to convince herself that she had imagined the attraction she had felt for Doug and the sparks that every touch had created. When that hadn't worked, she had told herself that there was a logical explanation for what she had felt. It was simple proximity and the romantic setting, akin to a classic shipboard romance. That argument had been so compelling that she had believed it. Until tonight.

This was not a romantic setting—at least not for the person who was serving as cook and dishwasher. But there was no denying the fact that the feelings she had experienced in Hawaii were happening again. They were real. Rebecca couldn't deny that. What she could do— what she would do—was ensure that they didn't grow. No matter how much he attracted her, no matter how many sparks flew, there was no ignoring the fact that Doug West was the last man on earth for her.

A man with a weak heart. Never again!

Rebecca loaded the silverware, then dumped soap into the dishwasher. As the machine started to fill, her son looked up from the corner of the kitchen, where he was playing with his beloved dachshund. Though he was healthy now, Rebecca knew she would never forget the scares she and Tim had experienced because of Danny's heart. They almost lost him twice before a very expensive surgeon worked the miracle that healed their son. That day, when the doctor had told them that the surgery was successful, Rebecca and Tim had been convinced that they had survived the worst life could offer. It was time for happily ever after. And, for a few short months, they'd had happiness, enjoying their son's newfound health and planning for Laura's birth. Then, without a warning, their peaceful existence had been shattered. Rebecca had been watching Danny playing in the backyard when the state police had called. Tim's car had crashed into a tree, killing him instantly. The autopsy revealed that he'd had a massive heart attack.

Biting her lip, Rebecca tried to fight the sorrow that always came with thoughts of Tim's death. Though time had lessened some of the pain, nothing could fully erase the memory of what she had endured. If she ever remarried—and Rebecca knew that it would be good for Danny and Laura if she did—it would be to the man with the strongest heart in Texas. Not a man who had just had a heart attack. Not Doug West.

Breakfast had reminded him of Hawaii. Doug settled back in the comfortable wing chair, his lips curving into a wry smile as he admitted that almost everything here reminded him of Hawaii. It wasn't as if the food was the same. There had been no tropical fruits or poi on today's menu, nor was the dining room open to the trade breezes the way the one at the Bradford had been. The similarity was in the overall ambience, the sensation of being a pampered guest and—most importantly—the presence of Rebecca. A man could get used to living like this.

Doug looked around the small library where he had

come after breakfast. The furniture was a comfortable mixture of antiques and newly acquired pieces, all of which were padded and upholstered. Unlike the rest of the inn, which boasted polished wood floors and area rugs, this room was carpeted. Doug suspected the floor covering, like the choice of furniture, was designed to minimize noise. This was a place where a person could read in peace. Judging from the wall of floor-to-ceiling bookshelves, either Rebecca enjoyed reading or she thought her guests would. Doug voted for the former. Lucky Rebecca. There had been a time in Doug's life when he read for pleasure. That time was long past. Now his reading consisted of emails, reports, and presentations.

He opened the file folder that had elicited frowns from Terri when he'd slid it into his laptop case. "You're supposed to be on vacation," she had told him, mimicking the doctor's words.

No matter what either of them thought, this was not a vacation. Other than that week in Hawaii, Doug West didn't take vacations. He had a business to run, and that business required his attention if not twenty-four hours a day, seven days a week, then close to it.

"Did you order a subscription to the *Wall Street Journal*?" Rebecca appeared in the doorway. The woman had no right to be so beautiful. The combination of that golden blond hair and those deep blue eyes made her look like the all-American girl. But Rebecca was not a girl. Far from it. She was a woman with a woman's soft curves and a hint of sadness that only added to her allure. Though normally Rebecca smiled, today she wore an expression Doug had never seen on her face.

The *Wall Street Journal*? "I didn't order it, but I imagine Terri did." It appeared that his assistant had bowed to the inevitable and admitted Doug would be working while he recuperated. "She promised me all the comforts of home."

Rebecca's lips curved, and this time there was no doubt what she was feeling. This could only be called an apologetic smile. "I hate to tell you this," she said with that soft Texas drawl Doug found so attractive, "but this morning's edition has been slightly customized by Doxy." Rebecca held out a wad of what might have once been a newspaper but whose center now appeared to be nothing more than soggy paper. Though Doug had never had a pet, he had a good idea what had caused the destruction.

"I gather that Doxy is a dog."

Rebecca nodded, her expression leaving no doubt that this particular dog's behavior was not what she expected of residents in her inn. "A dachshund."

"With a large appetite for newsprint." Doug completed the sentence.

"I'm sorry, Doug. I'd offer to get you a replacement, but I don't know where I'd find one this side of Kerrville, and I can't leave the inn today. It's Kate's day off."

That left Jim, but if Rebecca wasn't going to mention him, Doug wouldn't either. He shrugged. "I imagine that I'll survive. I can check the news online."

"Or skip it for a day."

"Now you sound like my doctor."

Rebecca's smile was as engaging as he'd remembered. "It seems that I keep falling into that role. You once called me Clara Barton."

"So I did." Doug glanced down at his arm. The short sleeve covered most of the burn. "There's not much of a scar left, especially compared to the ones the doctor gave me."

The blood drained from Rebecca's face, and for a second Doug thought she might faint.

"What's wrong?"

She shook her head. "Nothing." Her tone made it clear that she was lying and equally clear that she did not want to discuss whatever had caused her pallor. "I have rooms to clean." Rebecca dropped the mutilated newspaper on the desk, then hurried out of the room.

It was odd. If it had been another woman, Doug would have said that the thought of blood had bothered Rebecca, but he knew that that couldn't be the case. She had been as calm as could be when he'd set his arm on fire, not flinching at the decidedly unpleasant sights or smells. It had to be something else, but—try as he might—he could not figure out what that something could be.

Doug settled back in the chair and attempted to read the newspaper. There was no doubt that the unseen Doxy had made a mess of it. He probably should have taken his own advice and gone online, but Doug had never been one to shrink from a challenge, and reading this particular paper could only be called a challenge. Besides, although he wasn't sure why, right now the thought of booting his laptop held little appeal. Last night, for the first time since his surgery—perhaps the first time since he'd returned from Hawaii—his sleep had been undisturbed. And this morning, he'd enjoyed the leisurely pace of a multi-course breakfast. Now, when he ought to be checking sales reports and inventory projections or at least jotting down his thoughts for the "driver's road" ads, he was perfectly content to be sitting in a comfortably upholstered chair, reading a paper that was fit for little more than lighting fires . . . and then only after it dried. Which, judging from the moisture content, would be in a week or so.

Doug was puzzling over an article whose key paragraph had been chewed when he heard the commotion.

"Ucky! Ucky!" The high-pitched voice could only belong to a young girl, presumably the same girl whose rapid footsteps echoed on the hardwood floor. Doug raised an eyebrow. Bluebonnet Spring didn't appear to be the kind of inn that catered to children.

"Come back, Laura!" This voice was slightly deeper but still unmistakably that of a child. "Mom's gonna be mad."

"No!" the girl shrieked as she careened into the library, tripping on the thick carpeting and tumbling headfirst into Doug. "Ucky!" she declared as her small hands grabbed onto Doug's pant legs, leaving an ominous stain.

He couldn't disagree with young Laura's assessment. "Who might you be?" he asked as he disentangled her hands and rose from the chair.

Though Doug directed his question to the girl, it was the boy who'd followed her into the room, the same one who had predicted their mother's annoyance, who responded. "She's Laura and I'm Danny, and we live here," he said.

They lived here. That meant . . . Doug stared at the children, considering. Though the boy had dark hair and the girl was blond, there was no doubt they were brother and sister. There was even less doubt of their mother's identity.

The boy named Danny looked up at Doug. "You must be the sick old man who's staying for a long time. 'Course," he said after another glance at Doug's face, "you don't look so old."

"Thanks." Doug took note of the fact that Rebecca's son—for both kids' resemblance to her was unmistakable—did not tell him he didn't appear ill. Kids certainly knew how to deflate a man's ego.

Danny grabbed his sister's hand. "C'mon, Laura. Mom's gonna be mad that you bothered the man."

The little girl, who looked so much like Rebecca, screwed up her face as if trying not to cry.

"I won't tell." Rebecca didn't need to know that her daughter had mistaken Doug's jeans for a washcloth.

After Danny and Laura had scampered away, Doug

tossed the newspaper into a wastebasket and climbed the stairs to his room. First a husband, now two children. What other surprises did Rebecca Barton have in store for him? Doug grabbed the railing when he reached the landing, annoyed by the fact that a single flight of stairs had the ability to wind him. No wonder Danny thought he was ill. Doug tossed his folder onto the desk, then pulled out the chair.

He didn't claim to be an expert on kids. Heavens, no. He avoided them whenever possible. But, inexpert though he might be, he realized that these particular children were more than a year old. They must be from Rebecca's first marriage. No wonder she had gone to Hawaii! Though at the time he had believed that she had come to help forget her husband's death, Doug revised his assessment. With active children like that, it was clear she had needed a week away to recover. It was also clear why she had remarried. It can't have been easy raising two children alone. But Jim? Couldn't she have done better?

Doug shook his head. Rebecca, her husband, her children, and her dog were not his business. Apex was. Seconds later, he was listening to the phone ring a thousand miles away.

"Terri speaking."

"Good morning, Terri."

There was a fraction of a second's pause before his assistant said, "I thought you were supposed to be resting." Her voice radiated disapproval.

"And I thought you were supposed to be on my side." Doug kept his voice light, though he mimicked her tone. "Here's what I need. I didn't bring a fax machine, and I don't want to use Rebecca's . . ."

"Who's Rebecca?"

Doug frowned. Why on earth had he mentioned Rebecca? He should have remembered Terri's insatiable curiosity and her equally insatiable matchmaking. Of all the office staff, Terri alone had appeared pleased by his broken engagement, telling Doug that he and Lisa would not have been happy together.

"The innkeeper," he said shortly. "Married with two kids and one dachshund. Now, listen. I need the daily sales and inventory numbers emailed to me. Talk to Coolidge; he'll show you how to do it."

"But, Doug, the doctor said—"

"That I shouldn't be under stress. Not knowing how my company is doing will elevate my stress levels."

This time the silence was longer, and Doug could picture Terri's frown. At last she sighed. "I give up. You'll never change."

What was wrong with that?

Chapter Six

Doug bit into the peach cobbler. It was equally as delicious as the main course, something Rebecca called Mexican lasagna, had been. Even the vegetables, never Doug's favorite part of a meal, had been better than normal, and he'd actually asked for a second helping of both the parsnips and the lasagna. So had Jake, the other male guest.

Doug frowned. He and the anniversary couple, Jake and Mary, were still the only guests at the inn. That couldn't be good for Rebecca's cash flow. It was, however, good for Doug. Other than the children that morning, he'd had no interruptions. He had spent the afternoon reviewing the numbers Terri had emailed to him and had scheduled a teleconference with his ad agency for early next week. If Gina had been surprised to hear from him, she had hidden that better than Terri did. Gina had merely agreed that she'd coordinate the meeting and email him a dial-in number for the telecon, since one of the key members of her team was in Europe for three weeks. The wonders of modern technology. Though he hated not being in Detroit and working with his staff in person, Doug had to admit he had accomplished a lot today.

He swallowed a bite of dessert. The ice cream—correction, the low-fat frozen yogurt—had melted and blended with the succulent peaches, making a dish that was both delicious and, or so Rebecca claimed, healthy. Doug took another spoonful, trying not to dwell on the fact that for the foreseeable future he would be on a low-fat, low-cholesterol diet. Back home, that had sounded positively unappetizing, but Rebecca's cooking was changing his mind. Everything she had served had been flavorful, not the tasteless cardboard the words *low fat* had conjured in his imagination.

Doug hadn't been flattering Rebecca when he had told her that her meals were better than the Bradford's. They might not be haute cuisine, but they were exceptional. It was no wonder Rebecca had decided to open a country inn. The woman had a definite flair for both cooking and for making her guests feel at home. She had created an inn that combined comfort with luxury, resulting in a place that was part oasis, part cocoon, one hundred percent enjoyable.

Doug looked around the dining room, admiring the tasteful furniture and the garden view. Though it was not yet peak growing season, the formal garden was beautiful; not a leaf appeared out of place. Everything at Bluebonnet Spring seemed perfect, with one exception: Jim Locke. He was not the man Doug would have pictured as Rebecca's husband.

As he spooned the last bit of cobbler into his mouth, Doug tried not to frown. He wasn't sure what type of man he would have chosen for Rebecca. Though he ran through mental images of all the single men he knew, none of them seemed right. George didn't have a sense of humor. Harry didn't like children. Mike worked too much. Not one of them was good enough for Rebecca. Rebecca was special; she deserved a husband who was equally special. Doug savored both the last of the cobbler and the knowledge that in all probability, no one would meet the criteria he had established.

The anniversary couple rose and walked hand in hand from the dining room. They had told Doug they were celebrating their fortieth anniversary with a few days at Bluebonnet Spring. Though their gray hair and the lines on their faces bore witness to the length of their marriage, the smiles they lavished on each other made them look like honeymooners. Rebecca deserved someone who would love her the way Jake loved Mary.

Doug settled back in his chair and took a sip of coffee—decaf, of course—to camouflage his grin. Though he'd never been a parent, his reaction to Rebecca's husband was that of the stereotypical protective father. A second later his grin faded. Though he could joke about protective fathers, the truth was, Doug's feelings for Rebecca were not paternal. Not at all. He could claim that what he felt was simply friendship, but that wasn't true, either. What he felt was attraction, the attraction of a man for a woman.

Doug had been attracted to Rebecca in Hawaii. There was nothing wrong with that. The problem was, his attraction had not faded, even when he'd learned that she was married. Doug wasn't proud of that. He wasn't a man who harbored thoughts about another man's wife. No, indeed. He would remind himself, a hundred times a day if necessary, that Rebecca was Jim Locke's wife.

As the coffee suddenly seemed tasteless, Doug pushed his chair away from the table. If he wasn't going to think about Rebecca—and he wasn't—it would be easier to do that somewhere else, somewhere where he didn't see her, or hear her laughter, or smell the faint scent of her perfume.

It was an hour later when Doug admitted that the television, even though it had a hundred or more channels, held no appeal. The trade journals he'd brought were even less interesting, and the book that he'd picked up at one of the airport stores on the off chance that he'd have time to read failed to pique even a modicum of interest. Giving up, Doug grabbed a jacket and headed outside. Perhaps the crickets' serenade would be more soothing than the other forms of entertainment he'd tried.

The sun had set, but the full moon provided enough light that Doug doubted he'd fall into a gopher hole or stumble into the spring. It was, in fact, an ideal night for a stroll, if a man were so inclined. At home Doug's only nighttime forays were to and from his gym or a business meeting. Here, though, life was different. He found himself walking more slowly than he did at home, and for the first time in many months, he looked up at the stars. There was Orion. He had seen it in Hawaii, the night he and Rebecca had taken the sunset cruise. There had been a full moon that night too. Doug's steps slowed as he remembered the way the moon had glinted on Rebecca's hair and the fresh scent of that hair as they'd danced together, her head barely reaching his shoulders. He remembered how soft her hand had felt in his and how that silky blue dress had swirled around her legs. Most of all, he remembered the kiss they'd shared. Her lips had been warm and sweet and inviting.

Stop it! Doug admonished himself. *You're not supposed to be thinking of Rebecca. She's a married woman. Think of something—anything—else.*

As a car engine started, Doug turned, grateful for the distraction. The dome light was still on, revealing that the driver was Jim. The man waved, almost as if he were leaving for the day. In the doorway, Rebecca waved back. Doug raised an eyebrow, wondering where Rebecca's husband was going. Perhaps he had a meeting somewhere else. Perhaps Rebecca had sent him on a last minute errand. Whatever, it was none of Doug's business. He was taking a walk, getting the moderate exercise his doctor had ordered. That was all. Resolutely, Doug strode toward the spring. He wouldn't think about Rebecca and her husband. No, sirree.

Half an hour later, he began to retrace his steps. When he reached the spring, Doug saw a woman standing on the opposite side. Rebecca. There was no mistaking that blond hair or the petite frame. If he was going to adhere to his resolution not to think about Rebecca, to keep his distance from her, he should go the other direction. He would have done that. Of course he would have, if only she hadn't seen him. Turning now would be rude. That was the reason, the only reason, why Doug continued walking toward the woman who occupied far too many of his thoughts.

"I love this time of the day," Rebecca said when he was close enough that she had no need to raise her voice. "The children are in bed, and I have a few minutes of peace." In the distance, an owl hooted. Though the sound was melodic, it could not compare to the lilt of Rebecca's voice.

Doug nodded in sympathy. He knew how demanding a job could be. "I've heard that innkeepers are on duty twenty-four hours a day, every day." That was even worse than his own job.

It was Rebecca's turn to nod. "Close to that, especially when the inn is at capacity." This time her smile was wry. "So far I haven't had that particular problem, but since 'The Stockton Show,' reservations have increased. We're going to be full this weekend."

"That's good news."

"It certainly is. Even though I may not sleep all weekend, my banker will rest more easily, knowing that I'll be able to meet the next loan payment."

Her words brought back a host of memories for Doug. "I remember the early days at Apex. It wasn't the loans that worried me the most; it was the fear of not being able to make payroll." Doug had hated the fact that if he failed, other people would lose their jobs. That knowledge had increased his determination to succeed.

He and Rebecca were walking so close to each other that Doug could hear her intake of breath. "It was a nerve-wracking time," he told her, "but fun too, as odd as that may seem. I enjoyed the challenge of making the business successful."

"This is the first job I've ever had." Rebecca slowed her steps. Doug wasn't sure whether she was delaying their return to the inn or whether she feared that he would overexert if he walked more quickly. He hoped it wasn't the latter. For his own part, he was enjoying being with Rebecca. "I married right after college and became a stay-at-home wife," she continued.

Her last word jolted Doug back to reality. Rebecca was married, and he mustn't forget that. "Now you've got a new husband as well as your own business."

She stopped abruptly and stared up at him. "Husband?" The moon revealed the shock on Rebecca's face. She was looking at Doug as if he were speaking a foreign language. "Husband?" She repeated the question.

Could it be? Doug had never liked being wrong, but tonight was one time when he wouldn't mind it at all. "Did I misunderstand? I thought you and Jim were married."

Rebecca laughed, and surely it was only Doug's imagination that the laugh was self-conscious. "Jim's a good friend," she said slowly. "Just a friend."

Doug's day had improved a hundredfold.

Rebecca clenched her fist, then released it slowly, stretching each finger. She had told Doug the truth, but not the whole truth. If Jim had his way, he would indeed be her husband. But that was something Rebecca didn't want to discuss, particularly not tonight, and particularly not with Doug West. It was far too pleasant, just walking with him, enjoying the night air, the soft drone of the insects, and the scent of freshly mowed grass.

"Have you been back to Hawaii?" Rebecca changed the subject, hoping it would keep Doug from asking more questions about her.

"No." As he shook his head, she realized that his hair was longer than it had been a year ago. Did it feel as silky as it looked? Rebecca thrust her hands into her pockets. It was ridiculous, positively ridiculous, to be thinking of running her fingers through Doug West's hair.

"There was a convention in Honolulu," Doug said. "At the last minute I decided not to attend. I used the excuse that it was too far to fly, but the real reason I didn't go was because I knew it wouldn't be the same as our week at the Bradford."

Our week. Foolish though it might be, Rebecca liked the sound of that. Even more, she liked the fact that Doug's memories of that week on the Big Island seemed to match hers. "It was a wonderful week," she told him. There must be something about moonlight that encouraged confidences. Rebecca doubted Doug had told anyone why he hadn't attended the conference, and she hadn't planned to admit how often she thought of the time they had spent together. "The week was so much better than I'd expected, and that's all because of you."

Doug looked surprised. "You were the one who salvaged my trip," he said. "I meant to send you flowers as a thank you, but I got caught up in an emergency at the plant the minute the plane landed."

Even though he hadn't sent them, the thought of flowers made Rebecca smile. "There was no need," she said, "but thanks for the thought."

* * *

She was back in her room, brushing her hair, when the phone rang.

"I figured I should call before the weekend," her sister said after Rebecca had greeted her. "I knew you'd be busy then."

Rebecca settled into the wing chair and propped her feet on an ottoman. Conversations with Rachel were rarely brief. "I'm nervous about it." Though she wouldn't admit that to Jim or the others on her small staff, Rebecca kept few secrets from Rachel. "This is the big test." If the service wasn't what the guests expected, word would spread quickly, and people would start canceling their reservations. Rebecca couldn't let that happen. She wouldn't.

"You'll do fine. You always did work well under pressure." Trust Rachel to be her one-woman pep squad. Rebecca started to relax. Instead of gripping the chair's arms, her fingers stroked the velvet. It was soft. As soft as Doug's hair had looked.

Stop that! Rebecca admonished herself as she tried to listen to her sister. "Besides," Rachel continued, "your guests can't be any more difficult than Grandma Laura's bridge club."

Rebecca chuckled. "They were tough, weren't they?" She and Rachel had considered the elderly women the most demanding creatures on earth. One would claim that the tea was too hot. The woman next to her would insist that it was too cold. A third would point out a single speck of dirt in the corner of the fireplace mantel, even though Rachel had claimed the speck was actually on the woman's eyeglasses.

"The way I remember it," Rachel said, "they were never satisfied. But let's talk about more pleasant subjects. Did your long term guest arrive?"

Doug West was certainly a more pleasant topic than Grandma's bridge club. "He did."

Though Rebecca thought her words were noncommittal, she heard Rachel's intake of breath. "What's going on, sister dear? You managed to make two very ordinary words sound mysterious."

Rebecca shrugged. There was no point in not telling Rachel the basics. She wouldn't, of course, tell her everything. There were some things that even dearly beloved sisters had no need to know. "It really is a small world," Rebecca said. "I met him when I was in Hawaii."

"You what?" Rachel's voice rose an octave.

"I met Doug West when I was in Hawaii." Rebecca tried to repress her smile. She paused for effect, then delivered the bombshell. "I shared his honeymoon."

Her words were met with silence, a silence that lasted far longer than Rebecca would have thought possible. Rachel was never at a loss for words. If it weren't for the breathing that she could hear through the receiver, Rebecca might have thought her sister had dropped the phone. At last Rachel spoke, her voice choked with laughter. "I would not have believed it possible, but you've left me speechless. Tell me all about him."

"There's not much to tell."

"I beg to differ." Rachel chuckled. "It's all starting to make sense. Now I know why you seemed different when you came back from Hawaii."

"I was not different."

"You were." Once again, Rachel had to have the last word.

Rebecca was unloading the dishwasher when Jim arrived the next morning, his arms filled with grocery bags.

"They had a sale on Brussels sprouts," he said as he laid the sacks on the butcher block island. "I thought you might make them with the lemon sauce."

Rebecca nodded as she returned the last of the saucers to the cabinet. "That's a good idea." Jim knew that she liked to serve her guests fresh vegetables, and he had willingly served as a guinea pig when she had been experimenting with new recipes. "I'd better have green beans too, for the less adventurous guests."

"Like your children."

With a shrug, Rebecca reached for the first grocery bag. "Danny has decided that everything green is yucky. It started with peas, but now it's everything."

Jim handed her a can of baking powder. "It's a boy thing. I remember going through that stage myself. Look at me now. I eat everything." He opened a cabinet for Rebecca, his arm brushing hers lightly. "Rebecca . . ."

"We're full for the next four weekends," Kate announced as she entered the kitchen, carrying the reservations book.

"That's wonderful, Kate. I think it deserves a celebration." Rebecca pulled out three stemmed glasses and filled them with white grape juice. "To a full house!" she toasted.

When the phone rang and Kate hurried to the small office to answer it, Rebecca turned to Jim. "I don't know which news was better—all those reservations or the fact that Danny is simply going through a stage. I'm glad to know it will end someday."

"Not only that," Jim confirmed, "but sooner or later Danny will stop hating me."

Rebecca smiled, realizing how comfortable she felt with Jim. He was, as she had told Doug, a good friend, and like a good friend, he helped her keep her sense of humor. "He doesn't hate you." She put the last tin of tomatoes on the lazy susan.

Jim folded the empty bag and laid it on the pile of recycling. "Perhaps hatred is too strong, but you've got to admit that there's a mighty lot of resentment coming out of that boy. He doesn't want another man in your life."

Rebecca couldn't deny that. Her son had made it clear that he considered himself the man of the family. "Danny's been through too many changes in the past couple years. Between losing Tim, Laura's birth, moving here . . ."

"Is our lunch ready, Rebecca?" The wife of the anniversary couple poked her head into the kitchen. "Jake's anxious to go."

Rebecca handed her guest the picnic basket that she'd prepared while the dishwasher was running, then listened for a minute while Mary explained that she and Jake were going to the LBJ ranch today.

When the woman had left, Jim continued as if there had been no interruption. "I know that, and I want Danny to accept me. That's why I'm not going to push you, even though you know what I want to say. What I want to ask you," he corrected himself. "I can wait. I'm a patient man."

Patience, Rebecca mused, wasn't a word she would ever associate with Doug. She shook herself mentally, reminding herself that she was not going to entertain thoughts of Doug West. He was a guest, nothing more.

Seemingly oblivious to the direction Rebecca's thoughts had taken, Jim asked whether she had read the latest copy of *Today's Innkeeper.* She shook her head. "Not yet. Why?"

"There's a conference in San Francisco. I glanced at the agenda, and the sessions look good. I think you ought to go to it."

"Yeah, you ought to go." It was Fred, the member of Jim's staff who mowed lawns. He stood in the doorway, a grin on his face.

Everyone had told Rebecca how important it was to attend conferences, particularly when she was getting the inn started. The theory was great, but reality was something else. "I'm not sure I can leave Bluebonnet Spring," she said, "especially now that reservations are increasing."

"It's mid-week." Jim's voice was persuasive. "They have a number of workshops targeted for new innkeepers—building the business, finding the right market—things like that."

"I'll keep the grass mowed." Fred grabbed his thermos of iced tea and left.

"At last!" Jim looked at the now empty kitchen as if he didn't believe his eyes. "I thought the interruptions would never end."

"Why? Is something wrong?" Rebecca wondered what Jim had to say that couldn't be overheard by the staff. She stared at the man who had signed on as her landscaper, but had become both friend and advisor.

"Nothing's wrong," Jim assured her. If she hadn't known better, Rebecca would have said the way he ran his fingers through his sandy hair was a nervous gesture. "It's just that I won't have a minute alone with you until the weekend is over." His expression earnest, Jim took a step toward Rebecca. "I know you're worried about the weekend, but there's no reason. You'll wow all the guests."

"That's what my sister said. She gave me a pep talk last night."

"I can do better than that." Jim closed the distance between them and drew Rebecca into his arms. "What you need is a kiss for good luck."

He lowered his lips to hers.

As kisses went, it was pleasant. There was nothing wrong with it. There was also nothing special about it. Jim's kiss didn't set off any sparks, it didn't leave her fingertips tingling, and it didn't make her wish it would never end. Rebecca knew she wouldn't dream about it the way she did Doug's kiss.

Doug. Rebecca blinked in confusion. Why was it that everything reminded her of him?

Chapter Seven

They all arrived at once. It had to be Murphy's Law that six cars would pull up in front of the inn within thirty seconds, each one bearing guests who were obviously anxious to be settled in their rooms. Somehow, though check-in did not officially begin until two, they had all decided that the inn would welcome them an hour earlier. Rebecca, Doug knew, had just settled Laura in for her nap and was finishing her baking when the doorbell first chimed. He had dealt with irate labor unions, he'd persuaded skeptical boards of directors to accept his recommendations, and he'd negotiated contracts with notoriously difficult suppliers. He'd done all that, but he didn't believe he could have dealt with the onslaught of visitors that now filled the front porch and entry hall of Bluebonnet Spring. At least he wouldn't have dealt with them with Rebecca's aplomb.

The noise level escalated well past Doug's tolerance threshold, and his nose itched from the clash of too liberally applied perfumes. Had it been his company, Doug would have called in a phalanx of assistants. The problem was, Rebecca didn't have a phalanx of assistants to call.

She had only Kate, who wasn't due to arrive for another fifteen minutes, and Jim, who was—thank goodness—*not* Rebecca's husband but who also was nowhere to be seen.

Though the scene could only be described as chaotic, Rebecca appeared unfazed by it. She stood there, smiling at the elderly couple who, seemingly oblivious to the line of people behind them, were explaining for the third time that they were celebrating their golden wedding anniversary. "For the whole year," the woman said, repeating her husband's words.

From his vantage point at the far end of the parlor, Doug saw that Rebecca continued smiling, though the faint lines between her eyes told him she wasn't as calm as she appeared. Despite the fact that she seemed to be concentrating on the older couple, she couldn't be unaware of her other guests' impatience. Doug wished there were something he could do to help Rebecca, but she'd been adamant in refusing offers of assistance. He was, she had told him more than once, a guest.

"If you'll excuse me for a moment," Rebecca said to the older couple. "I'll be right back to show you to your room." Without appearing to, she hurried toward the kitchen, reappearing only a minute later, this time bearing a silver platter covered with chocolate chip cookies which she placed on a table in the parlor. Doug bit back a smile, watching the guests follow Rebecca as if she were the Pied Piper.

"I hope you'll all help yourselves to a cookie or two," she said to the people who were now milling around the parlor. "I'll get you settled in your rooms as quickly as I can."

The anniversary couple were the first to take cookies. "My dear, these smell as good as my mother's used to," the woman said, biting into the still warm confection. "Much better than those cookies they sell in the mall."

The cookies were, Doug realized, a masterful stroke. While Rebecca's guests had been on the verge of being annoyed by the delay, now they were talking among themselves, commenting on the cookies' flavor, and speculating on what would be served for dinner. The strain that he'd observed on Rebecca's face hadn't lessened, but at least it hadn't increased.

There was a sudden lull in the conversation, and Doug heard the unmistakable ping of a light bulb burning out. "Don't worry, Mrs. Mitchell." Rebecca's voice carried into the parlor. "I'll have that fixed before sundown."

As Rebecca returned to check in the next guest, Doug rose. He wouldn't ask; he'd simply solve the problem. After all, it wasn't brain surgery. He knew where she kept her supplies, and he certainly knew how to replace a light-bulb.

He was screwing the new bulb into the socket when Rebecca escorted the next guests down the hall. Doug saw her look of shock and the way she quickly disguised it. It was only after she had the new arrivals settled in their room that she returned to the hallway.

"What are you doing?" Though she kept her voice low, it was filled with emotion. Oddly enough, that emotion didn't sound like anger or annoyance, which is what he would have expected. It sounded like fear. That was, of course, absurd.

"I thought it was fairly obvious," Doug said in the voice he used to calm irate customers. "I was changing a light bulb." He stuffed the burned out bulb into his pocket and folded the stepladder. Perhaps if he acted as if this were a normal occurrence and not some extraordinary feat, the color would return to Rebecca's face.

"You shouldn't be doing that," she hissed.

"Why not? It's not union work, is it?"

"Of course not." Rebecca's lips turned upward as she appreciated the absurdity of his question. "But you're a guest."

"A guest who wants to help."

"What if you hurt yourself?" The same emotion he'd heard before was once again reflected in Rebecca's voice. This time Doug had no problem identifying it. "You're supposed to be resting." As absurd as it was, Rebecca appeared genuinely frightened, as if she thought that screwing in a single light bulb would trigger another heart attack.

"I'm not an invalid, Rebecca." And he most definitely hated being treated like one.

"Of course not." Though she tried to put conviction into her words, she could not disguise the trembling of her hands. Doug didn't want to stare. That would only make her self-conscious. Still, he was perplexed. It was one thing to be concerned about a guest's health—even a friend's health. This was more than concern; it was fear, pure, unadulterated fear. And that made no sense.

Rebecca's reaction was extreme. The question was, why? Short of confronting her, which he had no intention of doing, Doug doubted he'd learn the reason. It didn't matter, he told himself. After all, he was a guest here, nothing more. When the month ended, he'd return to Detroit, his path and Rebecca's diverging once again.

Doug frowned at the realization that he'd never see Rebecca again.

Several hours later, he stood in the parlor, mingling with the other guests as they savored Rebecca's hors d'oeuvres.

"This is a first class inn," one of the men said. He and his wife appeared to be the youngest guests, perhaps in their mid-twenties. Today the guests were all couples, none with children, and Doug was the only single person.

Doug nodded. "It certainly is first class. Rebecca has done a great job." Even though earlier that afternoon the parlor had been crowded with guests and luggage, now everything was restored to perfect order.

"If dinner's as good as these," the man's wife said, gesturing toward the miniature quiches, "we'll be coming back to Bluebonnet Spring."

Doug nodded again, pleased by the couple's reaction. That was what Rebecca needed, repeat customers. They and word of mouth were the best allies an innkeeper could have. "When I find a place that I like, I bring friends with me the second time." It was a lie. As someone who never vacationed, Doug had no experience introducing friends to spots like this, but a little white lie wouldn't hurt, particularly since it might help Rebecca.

"That's a good idea, honey, isn't it?" The woman took a tiny star-shaped sandwich from the tray.

While he appeared to agree, her husband's eyes narrowed, as if he suspected Doug's motives. "Are you one of the owners?"

"No," he assured them. "I'm just a selfish man. I want the inn to do well so that it'll be here for my next visit." Though the explanation was as false as his original statement about bringing friends with him, as he pronounced the words Doug found himself considering them. When the month was over, he didn't have to say good-bye forever. He could return to Bluebonnet Spring. It would, of course, simply be to support Rebecca, to help her occupancy rate. But though he told himself that, Doug didn't completely buy the explanation. What on earth was happening to him?

What was happening to her? Rebecca settled back in her rocking chair. The dishes were done, the children asleep. This was her private time, the time when she normally read a book or watched a little television. But today was different. No matter what she did, she couldn't stop thinking about Doug.

They hadn't spoken during dinner. With the inn at capacity, Rebecca was far too busy cooking to spend much time in the dining room. Other than her normal visit to each of the tables to greet the guests, she had remained in the kitchen. But each time she looked out, gauging the guests' progress, her gaze had met Doug's, and each time their eyes had locked, she had felt a frisson run down her spine.

It was ridiculous! She was acting like a teenager with a crush on a classmate. How absurd! Rebecca wasn't a teenager, and Doug wasn't a classmate. He was a guest. Theirs was a business relationship, nothing more. The man was here for a month, nothing more. Once he checked out, she would never see him again.

That was as it should be. Doug was handsome and charming and Rebecca enjoyed his company more than that of any man she'd ever met, but he was all wrong for her. It wasn't simply that he lived a thousand miles away. It wasn't that she doubted he was interested in a widow with two children and a brown dachshund. The real problem was, Rebecca couldn't let herself care about a man with a damaged heart. She couldn't and she wouldn't. Her brain knew that. Unfortunately, the rest of her was harder to convince.

"Going somewhere?" It was Monday afternoon. The last of the weekend guests had left, and Rebecca was heading toward her car, her determined stride branding her a woman with a mission. Doug rose from the porch chair, intrigued by both Rebecca's unexpectedly brisk pace and the way that pace made her silky skirt swirl around her legs.

"I'm driving into Kerrville," she said, obviously oblivious to the fact that he was admiring her. "My larder is literally bare."

There was no hint of invitation in her tone, but Doug didn't need one. "Mind if I tag along?"

Rebecca stopped in mid-stride and raised an eyebrow. "It won't be very exciting."

"All things are relative." The new ad campaign was in Gina's capable hands. Doug had finished reading both the *Wall Street Journal* and the local paper. He had never acquired a taste for daytime TV, and he wasn't interested in watching magpies compete for the birdbath. At this point the excitement quotient in his life was so low it was off the scale.

"Does that mean you're bored at Bluebonnet Spring?"

Though Doug thought he detected a hint of amusement in Rebecca's voice, he wasn't taking any chances. "*Relaxed* is the word I'd prefer to use." After what he thought of as "the lightbulb episode," Doug refused to discuss his health. Every time that topic arose, Rebecca acted as if he were an invalid. He wasn't, and even if he were, he wouldn't have wanted to be reminded of his infirmity.

"It looked to me as if your big weekend was a success," Doug said, deliberately changing the subject as he climbed into the passenger seat of Rebecca's minivan.

She started the engine, then turned to him with a smile brighter than the Texas sun. "I heard a lot of promises of repeat visits, and half a dozen people actually made reservations."

"That's great!"

"I thought so." Rebecca pulled onto the main road and accelerated. "I want so badly for Bluebonnet Spring to be a success," she said as she rounded the first curve. "I can't bear the thought of uprooting Danny again."

"I've heard that kids are resilient."

Rebecca's smile dimmed. "I prefer not to test that particular theory any further."

She drove well, obviously familiar with both the twisting

roads and the van. Sooner than Doug would have imagined, they were in Kerrville, loading shopping carts with
produce and canned goods. Though no stranger to super-
markets, Doug watched, amazed at both the quantity and
the variety of products Rebecca was buying. His thoughts
began to whirl.

"I need a dozen cans of tomato paste," she said, consulting her list, "and ten of those large cans of puree."

The whirling accelerated. By the time they were back in
the van, heading south toward the inn, Doug's thoughts
had coalesced into a plan. The proposal was next. He
turned toward Rebecca. "You bought a lot of groceries."
He wasn't sure how she would react to his ideas, and so he
tried to keep his voice neutral. It was crazy—totally
crazy—but he felt as if he had as much riding on her reaction as he had the day he'd convinced Apex's board of
directors to approve a major expansion.

"I may need a truck next time." Rebecca slowed for a
curve in the road. "The mini van is a great mom mobile,
but it doesn't have as much cargo space as I thought."

This was the opening he needed. If he phrased it prop-
erly, it wouldn't seem as if he were interfering in her business. "There could be another answer," Doug said as
casually as he could. "A way to save time and money and
not buy a truck."

He wasn't sure which part of the equation caught her
interest, but there was no doubt that Rebecca's eyes
reflected curiosity. "What do you mean?"

Wanting as much of her attention as possible, Doug
waited until the road straightened again before he spoke.
"Blame it on my background in finance, but I hate to see
people overpay."

"No one overcharged me." There was more than a hint
of defensiveness in Rebecca's voice.

"I didn't say they did. The problem is, you paid the

same price as someone who bought a single head of lettuce or one can of tomato puree."

They were passing through a wooded area now. Doug wasn't sure what kind of trees they were—perhaps pecans—but they certainly were pretty, especially with all those prickly pears around them. He'd have to ask Rebecca about them later. Right now he wanted to focus on her procurement policies.

"You're talking about bulk rate." The fingers that had tightened on the steering wheel at the thought of being cheated relaxed a little. "When I opened the inn, I asked the shopkeepers for bulk rates, and they refused."

Doug wasn't surprised. No one offered lower prices unless there was a compelling reason. "We could try a different approach. I saw three large stores on the way in, in addition to the one where you shopped." As Rebecca nodded, Doug continued, "What we'd do is prepare a list of common items that you buy and ask each of those stores to competitively bid on supplying them, including delivery."

Rebecca was interested. The light in her eyes told him that. "Do you think they'd agree?"

"Absolutely." The elation that surged through him was absurdly out of proportion to the topic. For Pete's sake, this was hardly a multi-million dollar deal. Why then did he feel so ridiculously pleased that Rebecca seemed to approve of his idea? "That's the way institutions work," he said in a voice that betrayed none of his excitement.

Though obviously intrigued, Rebecca frowned. "I don't know how to ask for a bid. I haven't gotten to that chapter in *Innkeeping for Dummies* yet."

Doug had never read the book, if in fact there was one by that title, but he'd issued many a Request for Quote, or RFQ as insiders abbreviated it. "Let me do it. It'll give me something to do besides read the *Wall Street Journal*."

"Which, I trust you've noticed, has not been chewed."
Rebecca's voice was light, her smile engaging.

"That fact has not escaped my keen perception. Now,
are you going to let me play?"

"That's your idea of play?" Though she continued to
smile, Rebecca didn't try to hide her sarcasm.

"I'm a workaholic, remember?" But when he returned to
his room and booted his PC, preparing to start Rebecca's
RFQ, Doug realized it had been three days since he'd
checked his email. Planning a vacation and forgetting
email. What on earth was happening to him?

The inn was unnaturally quiet, Rebecca realized the
next day as she unloaded the breakfast dishes from the
dishwasher. There was no sound of her children, their
dog, or Doug. Though Bluebonnet Spring was normally
quiet once the departing guests had checked out, ever
since Doug had arrived, she had always known that someone was inside. It wasn't that Doug made much noise. He
didn't. But Rebecca had sensed his presence. Not today.
Today the house felt empty, and that was odd.

As she did every few minutes, Rebecca glanced out the
window, checking on her children. This time what she
saw made her eyes widen.

Danny and Laura were in the sandbox. There was nothing unusual about that, since the sandbox was currently
their favorite place to play. Doxy was flopped on the
ground next to them. There was also nothing unusual
about that, since Danny rarely allowed the dog out of his
sight. What was surprising was her children's playmate.

"What happened?" Rebecca asked Doug when she
reached the edge of the sandbox. "I thought you were
inside working." That was what the man did each day,
even though she knew he was supposed to be resting. It
was true that the work he did wasn't physical labor, but

that didn't mean that it couldn't hurt him. Although, Rebecca admitted, Doug didn't look ill. If she hadn't known better, she'd have said he was a poster child for physical fitness. His dark hair, slightly tousled by the wind, highlighted a face that bore no hint of illness, and the short sleeves of his polo shirt revealed well-muscled arms. No one man had the right to be so handsome.

Danny tugged on Rebecca's hand. "Look, Mom." Her son pointed with pride at a pile of sand that had two turret-shaped extensions. "Doug is helping me make a castle."

"Mr. West is helping you," she corrected.

"Aw, Mom, he said we could call him that."

"Doug." Though Laura struggled with the name, there was no question of what she was trying to say. Outnumbered, Rebecca looked at the man who had turned into a sandcastle architect. "What happened? How did you get drafted for sandbox duty?"

Doug shrugged as if this were part of his daily routine. "I volunteered." He took a handful of sand and showed Danny how to shape it into the start of a drawbridge. "It looked like you needed some time without interruptions, so I thought I'd provide it."

"You didn't have to do that." Rebecca couldn't forget the first day when Doxy had chewed Doug's paper. As if that wasn't bad enough, Danny had admitted that Laura had used their guest's trouser legs as a washcloth. When Rebecca had offered to have Doug's pants cleaned, he'd refused, but his expression had told her that he regarded children as creatures from another, decidedly less civilized, planet. Yet here he was, voluntarily spending time with the savages.

"I know I didn't have to. I'm a guest." Doug repeated her words in such a mocking tone that Rebecca couldn't help smiling. "Maybe I wanted to."

"And maybe the moon is made of green cheese."

Danny shook his head. "No, Mom. That's not true. The moon isn't made of cheese."

As if in agreement, Doxy barked, then scratched in the sand.

"Okay, kids, Mr. West is going back into the house. It's coffee break time for him." In order to keep some measure of sanity, she had taught Danny that there were no interruptions when she was having a coffee break. Though she knew that the ten minutes she allowed herself probably felt like an eternity to her son, they helped revive her.

"I've heard the zoo in San Antonio is a good one," Doug said as he accepted a mug of steaming coffee. He waited until Rebecca was seated across from him before he continued. "I wondered if you and the kids would like to go there."

The zoo? Rebecca stared at Doug, not sure she'd heard him correctly. "Are you suggesting that you'd go with us?" The man might have spent an hour in the sandbox, but he had no idea what he was in for. Two excited children at a zoo for a whole day was far different from building a sandcastle. That was one of the reasons Rebecca hadn't taken Danny and Laura to the zoo; she'd been afraid that she couldn't control their enthusiasm. Visions of Danny racing off in one direction and Laura toddling in another were the stuff of nightmares.

Doug, however, had no experience with children, and so he had no fear. "You'll need to provide the car seats," he told Rebecca. "My rental didn't come equipped with them."

He was serious. He must be, or he wouldn't have thought about car seats. Rebecca took a sip of coffee as she considered the possibility of a day at the zoo. The idea was tempting. She had been so busy renovating the inn and getting it ready to open that she hadn't taken the children on any special outings. Rebecca had no doubt that they'd enjoy the zoo, and with Doug's help, she would too. The question was, would he? For someone unaccustomed to children, it could be a frustrating and exhausting experience.

"I'm not sure." Could she really ask this man to do that? Despite their week in Hawaii, he was now one of her guests. Innkeeping protocol probably prohibited extracurricular activities with guests.

As if he could read her mind, Doug said, "One thing you should know about me by now is that I don't issue invitations I don't mean."

Though he said nothing more, Rebecca knew he was referring to the invitation to share his honeymoon. She smiled, remembering how much she had enjoyed that week, then envisioned her children at the zoo. "In that case," she said, rising and sketching a curtsey, "I accept with pleasure."

The next morning, armed with Laura's stroller and diaper bag, toys for the car, and a change of clothes for both children, Rebecca led Danny and Laura outside. Despite her son's pleas, Doxy was locked inside the fenced-in area of the yard.

Doug raised an eyebrow, his surprise at the number of items needed for a one day excursion confirming that he had not spent much time around small children. Rebecca only hoped he wouldn't regret his offer by the time the day was over.

"Look, Laura!" Danny crowed when he saw that Doug had put down the convertible top. "There's no top to this car. But you gotta be good," he told his sister. "You can't cry." Laura, who apparently had no plans to cry, squealed with delight.

The open car was a brilliant stroke, Rebecca realized. The children were so excited by the novelty that they forgot to squabble. Danny even forgot to whine about leaving

Doxy behind, and he didn't ask how much longer it would be before they arrived more than a dozen times. For her part, Rebecca felt as if the wind was blowing away years of worry. Even if it was only for a few minutes, she felt young and carefree again. While her children played in the back seat, she and Doug sang along to the hits on the radio. Neither of them had perfect pitch, but it didn't seem to matter. What mattered was riding down the highway, enjoying the sun and the wind and the fact that for a few hours she was simply Rebecca Barton, not Bluebonnet Spring's innkeeper.

Rebecca was almost sorry when they reached the zoo, but as she buckled Laura into her stroller and saw Danny's eyes pop at the colorful posters, she knew that the fun had just begun.

"Mom lets me do that," Danny announced as Doug reached for Laura's stroller. "I'm a big boy."

"Indeed, you are," Doug agreed. Taking his cue from Rebecca, he let Danny push it for the first few yards. Soon, as she had known would happen, Danny tired of that, preferring to walk three feet ahead, then race back to report on the next animals.

Rebecca and Doug took turns pushing Laura. As if they'd done it a dozen times before, they matched each other's pace, and somehow Doug seemed to know instinctively which exhibits Laura would want to see. When they reached those cages, he would position the stroller so that she could stare at the animals. Even more amazing, Laura, who normally fussed at being confined to her stroller, rode without a complaint.

By the time they reached the large cats area, it was feeding time. It had been years since Rebecca had been at the zoo at feeding time, but she still remembered the thrill of watching the lions and tigers pacing and roaring, encouraging the keepers to bring their food. Laura, however, did not find it thrilling. Frightened by the roars, she started to cry.

Before Rebecca could react, Doug crouched next to the stroller. "They won't hurt you," he said in a kind but firm voice. "They're just hungry." Laura's eyes widened, and she stared at him. She was, Rebecca knew, preparing for another spate of crying, but then her brother interrupted.

Tugging on Doug's shirt, Danny announced, "Me and Laura are hungry too. When are we gonna eat?"

Rebecca frowned at her son. "Danny, that's not polite." When she had offered to bring a picnic lunch for them, Doug had refused, telling her that part of the appeal of a visit to the zoo was eating there, despite the dubious nutritional content of concession food.

"It's okay, pardner." Doug smiled at Danny. "What would you like?"

"Me and Laura like hot dogs."

"Hot dogs it is."

Apparently surprised by the easy acceptance, Danny said, "With French fries."

"Of course." Doug looked as serious as if he were negotiating world peace. "You can't have hot dogs without French fries."

"And ice cream."

Before Doug could agree to that, Rebecca intervened. "That's enough, young man. We'll see about ice cream after you and Laura finish your hot dogs."

As a mutinous expression crossed Danny's face, Doug said, "My mom used to have the same rules."

"Really?"

"Really."

Danny nodded, then started running toward the food stand. Seconds later he returned and looked up at Doug, his expression serious. "No peas. They're yucky."

To Doug's credit, he managed to suppress his smile. "I don't think they have any on the menu. You're safe."

Even without the yucky peas, both children managed to get about half their food onto their shirts, an event that appeared to bring them both great pleasure. "Doxy can lick it off," Danny confided to Doug, making Rebecca wonder if his spills had been deliberate. Though they were better behaved than she had expected, there was no doubt that Doug was getting an introduction to youngsters today. Rebecca was only thankful there was no cotton candy at this stand. That would surely have landed in Laura's hair.

When they reached the bears, Danny stared, obviously fascinated by the animals' antics. Laura began to fuss. Knowing her daughter's nap was overdue, Rebecca unfastened the buckles and lifted Laura from her stroller.

"I'll take her." Doug reached for the little girl, cradling her in his arms, then shifted her so she could see the animals. "Those are bears, Laura. Like your teddy bears." She stared for a moment, then turned, burying her face in Doug's chest and clinging to him. Rebecca looked at her daughter, startled by the unexpected behavior. Though Laura occasionally allowed Jim to hold her, it was clear that she was simply tolerating it. She had never clung to him. This was different. When Rebecca tried to take Laura from Doug, her daughter shook her head and tightened her grip on Doug.

They walked to the next cage, Danny leading the way, Rebecca pushing the empty stroller, and Doug holding Laura, who had fallen asleep in his arms. As they passed them, an older couple who sat on one of the shaded benches smiled.

"Look, Jed," the woman said to her husband. "What a handsome family."

It was an innocent remark. There was no reason why it

should have made Rebecca stumble or why the blood should have drained from her face. Family. One word. Three syllables. A simple concept. It was something she had always wanted, and for a few years, she had known that joy of being part of one. But that was the past. All she had now was a legacy of memories of how wonderful a family could be.

Rebecca stared at Doug. He and Tim were as different as two men could be. Tim had considered fatherhood his crowning achievement, while Doug lived for his business. Doug wasn't a family man, and today's trip to the zoo was no more than a pleasant interlude. Rebecca knew that. The problem was, today it had felt as if they were a family, and that was dangerous. Terribly, terribly dangerous. It wasn't simply herself she had to consider. She had survived heartbreak once; she would survive a second time. Her children were different. Though some might claim that the young were resilient, Rebecca was taking no chances. Danny and Laura were the most precious things in her life. She couldn't let them become attached to a man who was going to leave in three weeks. No, indeed.

Chapter Eight

Doug cradled the phone between his ear and his neck, making a mental note to order a headset. Though the desk in his room was remarkably well-equipped for a country inn, his neck was developing a definite crick from all the time he spent on the phone. He had issued the RFQ for Rebecca's grocery items and was now in the stage of responding to the stores' questions. Doug found it exhilarating seeing how similar and yet how different the process was from Apex's standard procurement. But this call and the next few he would make had nothing to do with Bluebonnet Spring.

"Good morning, Terri," Doug said when his assistant answered the phone. "Is Hal in?" It was the Apex production manager's urgent voice mail messages that had precipitated this call. Not wanting anything to intrude on Rebecca's time away from the inn, Doug had turned off his cell phone when he'd taken her and the children to the zoo, and he had forgotten to check his voice mail until this morning. The fact that normally unflappable Hal had left six messages, each with an increasing sense of urgency, told Doug the situation was critical.

"He's pacing around his office, waiting for you to call," Terri said, a hint of humor in her voice. "I'd never tell him this, but he reminds me of a lion in a cage."

Her words conjured the image of real lions, roaring out their desire for food, and Doug grinned. The excursion to the zoo had been more fun than he'd expected. While he wouldn't say he had dreaded it, there was no doubt that he'd approached the prospect of a whole day in the company of two small children with more than a modicum of wariness. Had it not been for his desire to help those children's mother, Doug would never have considered subjecting himself to it. After all, it was one thing to spend an hour in a sandbox, knowing he could walk away at any time, but quite another to commit to eight hours with no chance of reprieve.

To Doug's surprise the day had proven enjoyable. Though he had little prior experience with kids, he had discovered that he liked Rebecca's, even if they both appeared to believe that ketchup was a finger food. It had been amusing to watch Danny trying to act like a little man, and Laura was a sweetheart—a miniature version of her mother. Doug imagined she'd be a heartbreaker in another dozen or so years.

"Is there any particular reason Hal's upset?" Reluctantly Doug dragged his attention back to the present. He needed to be thinking about Apex, not one all too attractive innkeeper and her children.

"I'll let him tell you." The speed with which Terri transferred the call underscored the gravity of the situation. Normally she would have chatted for a minute or two, probably asking pesky questions about Doug's health.

"What's up?" Doug didn't bother with the niceties of small talk when he heard his production manager's voice.

"It's Johnson," Hal said, referring to a key supplier. "They claim they can't get us the fiber we need for the HPX filters until next week."

No wonder Hal was close to panicking. The High Per-
formance Extra was a new line of filters designed for the
luxury market. None of the other manufacturers had anything like it, and if Apex could be the first to market, they
had the possibility of capturing a lucrative market segment as well as a chance to enhance their image as a high-
end manufacturer.

"I assume you tried Wilcox," Doug said, referring to
the other fiber supplier Apex normally used. He reached
for his laptop and launched the production simulation
program.

"You bet." Hal's voice was strained. "They don't have
any extra inventory. Besides—"

"Their quality isn't the same." Doug finished the sentence. Hal was right. Even if Wilcox had been able to provide the material, Apex would have been taking a risk
using it for this particular filter. Too much depended on
the first batches being perfect to take that kind of risk. But
now, it appeared, there might not be a first batch, at least
not by the promised introduction date.

Doug started entering information into the laptop, his
fingers flying over the keyboard. "What day can Johnson
commit to a delivery?" As Hal gave him the information,
Doug continued his calculations. A minute later, the lines
between his eyes began to fade. "If we run three shifts for
a week, we can make it."

"But . . ." Hal started to protest.

Doug held up a hand to stop him, then realized that the
production manager couldn't see him. He knew that Hal
was going to point out that the plant normally ran only
two shifts and that union contracts prevented a switch to
three. Even if they could expand to three shifts, they
would be unable to find and train people to work the third
shift in time to resolve this crisis.

"Let's try this," Doug said. Though his plan was

unconventional, it wouldn't be the first time he had taken an unexpected route to success. "First we talk to the union stewards. If they agree, we'll call a meeting of the employees and explain the problem. We'll ask each shift to work twelve hours instead of eight. First shift will come in four hours early; second shift will stay four hours late."

Doug heard Hal's intake of breath. "But . . ." Even though it was only for a week, the extra hours would put a burden on the employees. Besides fatigue, there were all the personal issues that resulted from long work hours. Whole families would pay the price because one supplier was late. Fathers would miss their kids' ball games and mothers would have to scramble to find day care.

"We'll pay overtime for all twelve hours," Doug continued. "Not just the extra four."

Hal whistled. "There goes our profit."

"Let me worry about that. At this point, what's important is getting those filters delivered on time."

Two hours of back-to-back teleconferences later, the union agreed. Doug took a swallow of the coffee that had mysteriously appeared on the corner of his desk and started composing an email to all Apex employees, confirming the terms of their agreement and thanking them for helping to make the company successful. When he pushed the "send" button, he leaned back in his chair and stared out the window.

It was another of those beautiful days that he'd begun to consider characteristic of this part of Texas. Though he couldn't see her, he could hear a dog's excited yipping and knew that Doxy was outside, probably assisting Danny and Laura in sandcastle construction. Doug glanced at his watch, then frowned when he realized it was already noon and he'd missed the day's sandbox time. For reasons that he had never understood, the children rarely played in the sand after lunch. Doug's frown deepened when he realized that he regretted not being able to mix sand and water and help create lopsided castles. That was ridiculous. He had accomplished important things this morning.

Doug swiveled and faced the door, not wanting to look at the pastoral beauty of Bluebonnet Spring's lawn. He was glad he'd been able to resolve the production problem. There was no denying that. But something was wrong. The adrenaline rush and the almost euphoric feeling that normally accompanied a negotiation of this importance were missing, replaced by an inexplicable sense of emptiness. He should feel satisfied, but he did not.

The HPX filters were critical to Apex's continued growth. Doug hadn't been exaggerating when he'd told his employees that they would provide an entry into markets that had previously been closed and that the Apex name could become a household word as a result of these filters and the advertising campaign Doug had planned. Today he'd turned a potentially disastrous situation around, and all he felt was drained.

What was wrong?

"What's wrong?" It was Friday night, the inn was full, and Rebecca looked frazzled when Doug entered the parlor for the traditional appetizer buffet. He couldn't have said why he came down early tonight. Mingling with all those happily married couples only reminded him that he was the one person who dined alone, and so he had made a habit of joining the others for no more than the last fifteen minutes of the hors d'oeuvre hour. Tonight, however, he'd come to the parlor a few minutes before it started.

Rebecca, wearing the black skirt and simple white blouse that formed her dinner uniform, was arranging a platter of canapés. Though she kept a smile fixed on her face, Doug saw the lines of strain etched between her eyes. "We're going to have very slow service tonight," Rebecca said as she fanned a package of cocktail napkins, somehow turning those ordinary pieces of paper into a perfect circle. A container of multi-colored toothpicks would go in the center, making it look like a flower. Though Doug had seen the results each night, this was the first time he'd watched Rebecca create her beautifully appointed buffet table.

The table might be a work of art, but the artist was clearly unable to appreciate it. "Marie called in sick," Rebecca said, her eyes clouded with concern.

"Is she your waitress?"

Before Rebecca could respond, the first couple entered the room. Her friendliest smile firmly in place Rebecca greeted them and gestured toward the buffet. "I think you'll like the miniature quiches," she told another guest, continuing to greet people as they entered the room. The personal touch was one that Doug had heard several of the guests discussing, and from what he'd heard, the reaction was universally positive. People liked meeting their innkeeper.

"Marie's my one and only waitress," Rebecca admitted, keeping her voice low enough that she would not be over-heard. "She's so dependable that I haven't taken the time to recruit and train another. Obviously, a big mistake."

The words were out of his mouth before he had a chance to consider them. "Would you let me help?"

If the situation hadn't been so serious, Doug would have chuckled at the way Rebecca's eyes widened with surprise. "You know how to wait tables?" It was obvious that her image of him didn't extend to anything as practical as taking orders and serving food.

"I had a short stint in college." Doug chose not to tell Rebecca just how short that stint had been or the reason

he'd been encouraged to leave. "I don't imagine I've forgotten too much." And maybe this time he wouldn't spill
any hot liquids on a guest.

Though her expression was still skeptical, Doug knew
he wasn't imagining the fact that Rebecca had started to
relax. "Are you sure you want to?"

"Remember what I told you."

Before he could complete the sentence, she chimed in,
"You don't make offers you don't mean."

"Exactly."

"Then I accept." This time there was no doubt about it.
Rebecca was relieved.

"I didn't spill any soup," Doug announced with some
pride an hour later. The first hot liquid hurdle had been
passed. Hallelujah! He might not be fired—correction:
encouraged to leave—this job. "Everyone liked the soup.
But table four doesn't want onions on one salad, and six
says to skip the croutons."

The smile that lit Rebecca's face made Doug feel as if
he'd slain a dragon, not simply taken orders for salads.
"This is great! You're a lifesaver."

"Wait until the end of the meal before you make any
rash statements. You never can tell when I'll overturn a
glass or catch my sleeve in the candle flame."

"Don't even think about that," she announced, those
lovely blue eyes sparkling with mirth. "I'm too busy to
play Florence Nightingale."

"Or Clara Barton." As memories of the way they'd met
flashed through his mind, Doug started to laugh. Rebecca
appeared to have the same memories, for her smile turned
into laughter.

Though he would not have admitted it to Rebecca,
Doug considered it nothing short of a miracle that he
made no faux pas while serving. It was even more surprising that he enjoyed the experience. If truth were told,

though, it wasn't the experience of serving dinner to appreciative guests that he enjoyed as much as working with Rebecca. She was an amazing woman. Doug couldn't imagine anyone else he knew cooking for a crowd and enjoying it. Lisa had declared that dinner parties were for no more than six, and even then, they had been catered. But here was Rebecca, cooking a number of entrees for twenty guests and apparently having fun doing it.

"Where are Danny and Laura?" Doug had wondered why there was no evidence of them at dinners, since he knew they ate breakfast in the kitchen. It was the reverse of the adage that children should be seen and not heard. Though they were invisible to the guests, Laura's occasional squeal of delight and Danny's favorite epithet, "yucky," were audible, even when the door was closed.

"I have a babysitter." Rebecca slid a pork chop onto a plate. "Thank goodness she came tonight. It must be a phase of the moon or something in the water, because both kids were antsy today." Rebecca spooned applesauce next to the meat. "I suspect they're driving Susan crazy, watching Disney videos in slow motion or building Lego skyscrapers on top of her shoes."

The fond smile on her face told Doug just how much Rebecca loved her children. "They're great kids," he said. It was what every parent wanted to hear, but in this case it was also true.

The smile turned into a grin. "I think so, but I just might be prejudiced." A shadow darkened Rebecca's face, and she turned away slightly, spending more time than usual selecting a sprig of parsley to garnish the plate. "I wish their father could see them."

"He'd be proud of the way you're raising them." Doug offered her the only consolation he could, his heart aching for the pain she was enduring. Though he had no experience with parenting, Doug had heard enough people discuss it to know how difficult it was to be to be a single parent, yet Rebecca seemed to do it effortlessly. Normally she gave no sign that juggling innkeeping and motherhood was a tremendous feat, but tonight she'd let her guard slip. Tonight she'd revealed the sorrow that appeared to lurk so close to the surface. How Doug wished he could erase that sorrow. How he wished he could fill the voids in Rebecca's life.

He took the tray of plates Rebecca had prepared and headed for the dining room. They had guests to feed. But though his feet moved mechanically, Doug's thoughts continued to whirl. Rebecca was a woman who was meant to be married. A husband would ease the sorrow and fill the voids. He'd bring her joy, and in return he'd receive far more than he gave. The man who married Rebecca Barton would be the luckiest man on earth.

Doug wasn't that man. Of course he wasn't. His life was in Detroit with Apex, and Rebecca's was here. With Jim. Though he kept a social smile on his face as he served the entrees, inwardly Doug frowned. He'd seen the way the man looked at Rebecca. Jim wanted to marry her. That was good. That was what Rebecca needed. It was what Danny and Laura needed. It was even what Bluebonnet Spring needed. Doug knew that. He also knew that he shouldn't care that she would soon be Jim's wife, that Jim would be the man who saw her smile each day, the one who shared her life. That was the way it had to be. There was no point in wishing otherwise.

Rebecca laid the mug of herbal tea on the porch floor as she settled into the swing. The dishwasher was loaded and running, and she wanted a few minutes to relax before she went upstairs. She set the swing to moving slowly, then leaned back and closed her eyes. It had been a hectic evening, but—despite her initial worries when Marie had called her—it had turned out well. Not just well, it had been fun. Though it was the first time she and Doug had worked together, they had developed a rhythm after the first few minutes, as if they'd been serving meals together for years. And that surprised her. She had no doubts that Doug was a master in the boardroom, and if he were pressed, she guessed that he could have taken any one of his workers' places on the assembly line. But serving a meal? She hadn't expected him to be an expert at that.

"Do you mind if I join you?" As if she had conjured him, Doug appeared at her side.

Rebecca smiled as she looked up at him, then patted the seat next to her. "Aren't you afraid I'll rope you into more chores?"

He started the swing to moving again. "As I recall, I wasn't drafted. I volunteered."

"Thanks again." Doug's assistance had turned what might have been a disaster into a highly successful meal. She'd heard a couple of the other guests joking with him about his new job. Another man might have found the situation awkward, but Doug had parried the comments with grace, seeming to enjoy the banter.

"I was glad to help." He sounded as if he meant it. The porch light showed Rebecca that Doug's expression had changed. For once, he appeared unsure of what he was going to say. "This is probably going to sound like I'm trying to interfere," he said, "but it seems to me that you need to schedule some time off. You'll burn out otherwise."

"We went to the zoo," she reminded him.

"Yes, we did, but you admitted that that was the first break you've taken since you moved here."

Rebecca couldn't deny the truth of his words. "Maybe I'm a workaholic and thrive on this schedule." And maybe if she told herself that enough times, it would become true.

Though the light was muted, Rebecca could see that Doug's smile was wry. "You're not a workaholic. As a prime example of the species, I know the difference between someone who's working because it's what she needs to do to live and someone who lives to work."

It was true that Rebecca wished she could work fewer hours. Each day she felt guilty about the amount of time she didn't spend with her children. But she wanted to succeed at innkeeping. It wasn't simply for financial reasons. She and the children could have lived on Tim's life insurance. The truth was, Bluebonnet Spring was more than a business. It was Rebecca's chance to prove to herself that she could run a business, that she could be self-sufficient. Yes, things were tight financially right now, but soon the inn would be well enough established that she'd be able to hire more help. That would give her the time off that Doug was recommending.

"I'm going to a conference in a few weeks." Rebecca had sent in the reservation money two days ago, even though she still doubted the wisdom of leaving Bluebonnet Spring at this point in its existence.

Doug shook his head slowly. "That's still work, Rebecca. It may be a different kind of work, but don't kid yourself into thinking it's a vacation or anything that resembles one. You'll come home even more tired than if you were here."

Rebecca didn't doubt that. There were workshops all day and a trade show every evening, touting new products and services. Then there was the famous networking, which was reputed to last until late each night.

"You need to schedule at least one day a week when you don't work," Doug continued.

It was a nice theory. "I can't do that, Doug. Maybe a

year from now, but I'm still building the business right now."

"Half a day then."

Despite herself, Rebecca smiled. "You don't give up, do you?"

"Nope!" There was pride in Doug's voice. "I don't want you to wind up with a severe case of burnout. Nothing's worth that."

His words jolted Rebecca back to reality, reminding her of the reason he was here. He wasn't simply a guest. He was a man who was recuperating from a life-threatening illness. For a while, she'd forgotten. For a while, she had regarded Doug as a friend, a very special friend. How foolish could she be? Hadn't she learned her lesson?

"This is good." Jim swallowed a bite of lunch and smiled at Rebecca. "What do you call it?" It was Wednesday, the day that he always came to the inn for lunch. Although he occasionally dropped in for other meals, Wednesday was the day that Rebecca tried out new dishes, and Jim had volunteered to be her taste critic.

"It's a chicken salad wrap." Rebecca gestured toward the platter of sandwiches. "I like the color contrast of the tomato tortillas with the chicken. What do you think?" One of the lessons Rebecca had learned was that food had to look as good as it tasted, particularly in the hospitality business. "I'm considering having a soup, salad, and sandwich buffet one night a week," she explained, responding to Jim's unspoken question of why he was being served a sandwich rather than a traditional entree.

"Are you sure a buffet is a good idea? Don't most people prefer being served?"

"Actually, variety is what they like. At least that's what Doug claims." Rebecca tried to ignore Jim's frown. As long as it wasn't related to the food, she would pretend she hadn't noticed his disapproval. "I thought I'd try the buffet for a couple weeks and see what the reaction is. One thing's for sure, it'll be easier on the staff." Including herself. Rebecca suspected that that had been part of the reason Doug had made the suggestion. But, even if his primary motive was to lessen her workload, the idea had merit.

Jim nodded, washing down a bite of sandwich with a swallow of iced tea. "Speaking of staff, I told the guidance counselor at the high school that you were looking for a new waitress."

Rebecca took a deep breath, trying to control her temper. He meant well, she told herself as she pleated her napkin between her fingers. "I wish you hadn't done that," she said as mildly as she could.

"Why not?" Jim reached for one of the BLTs that Rebecca had wrapped in a spinach tortilla. "You told me you planned to hire someone else."

"I do," she agreed. It was ridiculous to be annoyed with Jim. He was her friend. Not just an ordinary friend, but one who had helped her in countless ways as she'd gotten the inn started. "I thought I'd look for someone older. I know there are a number of women who would like to work part time. This could be ideal for them, and I wouldn't have to worry about them going away to college or finding full-time jobs."

"Most people prefer younger wait staff." Jim's words sounded like an official pronouncement.

"I'm not so sure about that," Rebecca countered. "But Marie's young. If I hire someone a bit older, I'd be able to see how the guests react. You could call it a controlled experiment."

Jim raised an eyebrow, his skepticism apparent. "Did one of the innkeeping books tell you that?"

"No, Doug did." Rebecca glanced out the window toward the small playground. Doug was pushing Laura on the swing, while Danny built yet another sandcastle.

As Jim followed Rebecca's glance, she saw him frown. "How much longer are we stuck with that man?" he demanded. His normally calm voice seethed with anger.

Rebecca stared at the man who had been an important part of her life for the past year. If she hadn't known better, she would have said that Jim was jealous of Doug. But Rebecca did know better. Both she and Jim knew that there was no reason on earth why Jim should be jealous of one of their guests. Of course there wasn't.

Chapter Nine

It was the quiet time of the morning. The few guests who were leaving had checked out and new guests wouldn't arrive for another couple hours. Breakfast was over, and lunch for Danny and Laura was simmering. Though the day was overcast with rain threatening, both children were outside, playing with Doug. That left Rebecca free to plan menus for the weekend.

She opened a third cookbook, looking for inspiration. This was going to be another weekend with no vacancy, the kind every innkeeper loved and dreaded. If all went well, word of mouth would help fill the inn on future weekends. If, however, there were glitches, the news would travel by supersonic speed. Rebecca knew that. And that was why she was agonizing over which appetizers she should prepare. The mini quiches were a proven hit, but they were—Rebecca searched for the right word—predictable. Perhaps if she filled them with spinach instead of the normal ham and swiss, her guests would like them and consider them unusual, but not too unusual. Her clientele wasn't overly adventuresome.

Tapping her pencil thoughtfully, Rebecca turned another

page in the cookbook. The small egg rolls might work. Her ears perked at the sound of car tires on gravel. It was too soon for Jim or Kate to arrive, and she wasn't expecting guests. It could simply be someone turning around or who needed directions, but there was always the possibility of walk-ins. Her welcoming hostess smile firmly in place, Rebecca opened the front door and walked onto the porch. As she recognized the car and the woman who emerged from it, her blond hair artfully tousled, her jeans and T-shirt so perfectly fitted that they undoubtedly bore designer labels, Rebecca's smile faded.

"Rachel! What's wrong? Why are you here?"

Moving with the grace Rebecca had always envied, her sister climbed the steps and enfolded her in a hug. "I love you too, big sis," Rachel said as she kissed Rebecca's cheek. "But don't worry. I'll remember this warm welcome when I'm choosing your birthday gift."

As relief washed over her, Rebecca took a deep breath. "I'm glad to see you, Rachel. It's just that I hadn't expected you." And surprises, at least in Rebecca's experience, were rarely pleasant. "What brought you out here?" *And where is the baby?* Though Rebecca didn't ask the question, she saw no evidence of a child in her sister's car.

Rachel laughed and followed Rebecca into the kitchen. "Scott has this bet going with Luke," she said, referring to her husband and his best friend/former partner. "They're trying to prove who's the better father."

Rebecca raised one eyebrow, encouraging her sister to continue as she poured her a glass of iced tea. Rachel took a sip, then said, "Luke's wife went to some kind of retreat and took Alexa, leaving him with Adam. When he heard about it, that crazy husband of mine claimed Luke wouldn't survive three days as a single parent." Rachel laughed. "One thing led to another, and now Scott's home with Mary, trying to prove that he can out-parent his buddy."

It sounded like the kind of scheme Scott would enjoy, a bit like the first months of his marriage to Rachel, when the entire town of Canela watched the apparently mismatched couple, waiting for signs of a rift. Rebecca could picture Scott's eagerness to best his friend. The only part that she didn't understand was her sister's calm demeanor. "And you trust him with the baby?" Rachel might love her husband dearly, but she had never left him in charge of Mary for more than a few hours. "I'm afraid he'll powder the wrong end," she had once confided. But today the previously nervous Nellie appeared calm.

Rachel patted the cell phone clipped to her belt. "Let's just say that I'm keeping this turned on and the car filled with gas."

"Wise woman! I'm really, really, really glad you're here."

Rachel laughed. "Thinking about that birthday gift, huh? Seriously, sis, I'm planning to enjoy the next few days. I have every intention of spoiling that niece and nephew of mine." She took another sip of tea, then gave Rebecca an arched smile. "And, naturally, as long as I'm here, I want to meet your mystery man."

"Who might that be?" Rebecca couldn't help smiling with pleasure. The pleasure was, of course, due to the fact that her voice didn't betray any special interest in the person Rachel referred to as her mystery man.

"You can't fool me." Rachel wagged a finger at Rebecca. "I saw the way your eyes sparkled when all I did was mention him."

"Is there a law against sparkling eyes?" It had always been difficult to hide things from Rachel. The best thing was to pretend that Doug was an ordinary guest, that the thought of him didn't cause Rebecca's pulse to accelerate.

"He will be leaving in a couple weeks." Seventeen days to be exact. Somehow, although Rebecca wasn't sure how it had happened, almost half of his stay was over. "I won't see him again after that."

Rachel didn't appear convinced. "If you say so, sister dear."

Before Rebecca could find a suitable response, her son burst into the kitchen. "Mom! Mom! Me and Doug made a—" Danny skidded to a stop and stared at the visitor. "Aunt Rachel." He looked around the kitchen, obviously searching for someone. "Where's Uncle Scott?" he demanded.

Laughing, Rachel put her arms around her nephew and gave him a quick hug. "I guess I know where I stand. Now, let me see how much you've grown."

Danny took a step backward and stretched his neck, trying to add another inch to his less than impressive height.

Though she couldn't help smiling at her son's antics, Rebecca fixed him with what she called her "Serious Mom" look. "Say 'hello' to Aunt Rachel," she directed her son. "She made a special trip to see you and Laura." And Doug. Knowing Rachel, especially Doug. Rebecca wouldn't discount the notion that Rachel had suggested the whole scheme to Luke's wife, simply so she'd have an excuse for coming to Bluebonnet Spring.

"Uncle Scott couldn't get away this time," Rachel explained.

Danny shrugged. "That's okay," he told her with an engaging grin. "Me and Laura got Doug now."

As her sister gave her a look that said she wasn't buying Rebecca's "Doug is just a guest" story, Rebecca couldn't deny the sinking feeling that settled in her stomach. Her children had grown attached to Doug, making him part of their daily life. That was a problem. A huge problem. What would they do when Doug left? What would she do?

Rebecca had to admit that it was pleasant having Rachel visiting. Perhaps Rachel was simply enjoying being an aunt, or perhaps it was that she missed having her own daughter close by. Whatever the reason, Rachel was spending a lot of time with Danny and Laura, freeing Rebecca for paperwork. While paperwork was most definitely not her favorite way of spending a day, having it done would help her sleep that night.

She entered the most recent grocery bill into the accounting system, watching as the one entry updated the various accounts. Thank goodness she hadn't had to devise a system of her own! The software package had been both reasonably priced and remarkably easy to use.

"Do you mind an interruption?"

Rebecca swiveled at the sound of Doug's voice and clicked to save her work. "Not one bit. Besides," she admitted, "that was my last entry."

Doug sank into the chair on the other side of the desk, leaning back and crossing his ankles, the picture of a man of leisure. "Your sister is very nice," he said.

Rebecca raised an eyebrow. "I agree, but somehow I doubt that Rachel's the reason you're in my office." He had been careful not to interrupt her during the half hour a day that she had declared "office time." The fact that he was here today and that he was making such a show of being relaxed told Rebecca there was an ulterior motive.

"You're right about that." Doug uncrossed his legs and leaned forward ever so slightly. "I have two questions for you."

"What if I don't have the answers?"

"Don't worry, Rebecca. It's not a test." He leaned forward

a little more, his brown eyes serious as he said, "I've been thinking about ways you could fill the inn mid-week."

Rebecca was intrigued. Almost any innkeeper would agree that mid-week occupancy was a challenge. Weekends were the traditional time for people to visit an inn, and enough managed to wrangle long weekends that Monday and Thursday nights weren't too bad. But Tuesday and Wednesday were sometimes "total vacancy" nights.

"Do you have any suggestions?"

"A couple. And that's my first question. I wondered if you had considered targeting some San Antonio companies for publicity?"

The truth was, Rebecca had done only limited publicity, and all of that had been geared for the leisure market. She hadn't targeted businesses, but that didn't mean that she wouldn't. "What would the angle be?"

"I have two different ideas." Doug pulled a sheet from his back pocket and handed it to Rebecca. It was, she saw, a list of company names, addresses, contacts, and phone numbers. "These have R&R—" When she raised an eyebrow, he explained, "Reward and recognition programs for their employees. Normally, that's a gift certificate or tickets to a show. I thought a couple nights here mid-week might be a nice alternative to that. I imagine you could offer the companies a healthy discount off your rack rate and still make a profit."

Rebecca nodded. "You're right. My biggest costs are simply keeping the inn open. Utilities, the mortgage, insurance. Extra guests don't raise the incremental costs significantly." She did a quick mental calculation. "Even at a fifty percent discount, each night would help pay some of those fixed costs."

"Exactly." Though Doug kept his voice neutral, Rebecca recognized the satisfaction in his expression. He looked almost as pleased as he had the day she'd agreed to let him issue an RFQ for her groceries.

"That idea was a winner," she told him. "What's the second?"

"Some companies conduct off-site meetings," Doug said, pulling another sheet from his pocket. "They'll do team building or confidential planning sessions somewhere away from corporate headquarters, then have the people stay overnight to help them bond. Why not have those meetings here? You could turn the parlor into a conference room without too much trouble."

Rebecca didn't even try to hide her enthusiasm. "That's a great idea!" It would be wonderful if she could increase her mid-week occupancy rate. And even though Doug hadn't mentioned it, there was always the possibility that some of the people who came to Bluebonnet Spring on business would return for pleasure.

She studied the two lists. Doug, it appeared, had done his homework, providing her with names of not just the largest companies in San Antonio but also smaller companies and branch offices of national firms. "I ought to put you on the payroll. Seriously, though, Doug, how can I thank you?"

His grin reminded her of the proverbial cheshire cat. "That was the perfect segue to my second question." He paused for effect. "You know I think you work too hard. If you really want to thank me, take an evening off." He paused again. "Drum roll, please." Another pause. The man definitely liked drama. "And, now for the second and final question. Will you spend that evening off with me?"

Startled, Rebecca blurted out the first words that came to her head. "A date?"

This time it was Doug who looked a bit startled. "Date might be a four letter word, but it's not a disease." He gave her a smile that was designed to ease her worries. "You

can call it a business meeting if that'll make you feel better. I don't care, so long as you say 'yes.'"

She probably shouldn't. After all, hadn't she told herself she couldn't let herself grow attached to a man who
was leaving? But it was so very tempting. Rebecca
remembered the days she and Doug had spent together in
Hawaii and how magical it had been. It would be wonderful to recapture at least a portion of that magic for an
evening, and since Rachel was here, she wouldn't feel
guilty about leaving Danny and Laura with a babysitter.

"Yes," Rebecca said. "I'd like that." Then, just so she
could watch Doug grin, she asked, "Where are we going
to have that business meeting?"

"It's a surprise, but if you still have the dress you wore
on our last night in Hawaii, you could wear that." Almost
before she knew what was happening, Rebecca had agreed
that they'd have their "business meeting" the next day.

"I think it's romantic," Rachel said as she zipped
Rebecca's gown, then stood back to admire her thirty
hours later. It had been Rachel who had insisted Rebecca
wear long, dangling, rhinestone earrings and who had
spritzed her favorite perfume on Rebecca's pulse points.

"You have an overactive imagination." Though
Rebecca thought Doug's plans were romantic, she had no
intention of admitting that to her sister, just as she had no
intention of admitting that she liked the way the earrings
looked and felt. "Doug told me to pretend this was a blind
date," she said, shaking her head slightly. The earrings
bounced against her cheeks. "How can I do that, when I
never had a blind date and don't know anyone who did?"

"It would have been difficult to have a blind date in
Canela, where everyone knew everyone else. I had a couple when I lived in Dallas." Rachel wrinkled her nose.
"The less said about those, the better." She straightened
the back of Rebecca's gown. "I guess you're going to

have to use your imagination." Rachel chuckled. "I'll be using mine all night, trying to figure out where you've gone and what you're doing. Then again, maybe I'll just ask Doug."

But when he descended the stairs, dressed in a business suit and tie, all Rachel said was, "Be sure to wear your seat belt, drive carefully, and have Rebecca home by midnight."

Rebecca gave her sister a quizzical look. "Are you practicing for when Mary's a teenager?"

"You bet! But I'll tell you something I might not tell her." She lowered her voice to a stage whisper. "Have fun!"

Laughing, Rebecca and Doug descended the front steps, waving good-bye to the children. As he opened the door and ushered her into the car, Doug murmured, "You're beautiful."

So are you. Though the words were on the tip of Rebecca's tongue, she did not utter them. Doug wouldn't appreciate her telling him that he was beautiful. Men didn't seem to like that term. Beautiful, handsome—it didn't matter which word you used. The simple fact was, Doug was the most attractive man she'd ever met. She turned in her seat, angling so that she could see him better. Tonight was a night for the memory books, and Rebecca was going to do her best to remember every detail.

"I don't suppose you're going to tell me where we're going." All she knew so far was that they were headed toward Kerrville. Rebecca figured their destination was someplace fancy, or Doug wouldn't have suggested the long formal gown and insisted on keeping the convertible top up so that she wouldn't get windblown. But, for all she knew, he might be taking her to a fast food restaurant, and the gown was part of the effort to surprise her.

"It wouldn't be a blind date if I told you."

"I thought a blind date was when you didn't know the other person."

Feigning innocence, Doug said, "Really?"

"That was the commonly accepted definition in Canela."

"Well, then, we'll have to redefine the term." As they pulled into a parking lot on the outskirts of Kerrville, Doug turned to Rebecca. "Close your eyes."

"Why?"

"How can it be a blind date if you can see?" When she closed her eyes, she heard a soft sound, then felt the smooth texture of silk being draped over her eyes.

"What are you doing?"

Doug knotted the scarf at the back of her head. "Just making sure you don't peek. I don't want to spoil the surprise."

Rebecca heard him roll down his window and leave the car. Then, deprived of sight, she found her ears attuned to noises that she might otherwise not have noticed. Children called for their parents, adults raised their voices as they spoke into cell phones, cars honked, a horse clip clopped . . .

A horse! Rebecca tipped her head to the side, listening. Though riding was one of the favorite pastimes in the Hill Country, it was unusual to hear a horse in this part of the town. The sound was nearer now, and it seemed to be accompanied by the sound of wheels. She sniffed. No doubt about it. There was a horse, and it was very, very close. She could smell it, and if she listened carefully, she could hear its breathing. If she had to guess, she would have said that the horse was standing in the space next to Doug's car.

A second later Rebecca's door opened, and the smell of horse was overwhelmed by the spicy scent of carnations.

They were one of her favorite flowers, partly because of their delicious fragrance.

"Hold out your left hand," Doug said, then fastened the corsage on her wrist.

Flowers. Rebecca smiled, remembering that the last time she had worn flowers had been in Hawaii. Doug had given her those too. "Oh, Doug, they smell wonderful." She raised her hand to her face, feasting on the fragrance. "I want to see them."

The horse snorted, as if he understood.

"All in good time." Doug recaptured Rebecca's hand and drew her out of the car. When she was standing, he led her a few feet. They were closer to the horse now. Not only was the smell stronger, but Rebecca could feel the animal's warmth.

Doug whisked the scarf from her eyes, leaving Rebecca to blink at the bright sunshine. As her eyes adjusted, she smiled, for she was standing within touching distance of the most beautiful horse-drawn carriage she had ever seen. The coach, which was designed for two, was constructed of gleaming black wood with fanciful gold trim. The leather top was folded back, revealing golden upholstery. A single gray horse, the one she'd heard and smelled, stood in front of the carriage, his harness covered with black and gold designs that matched the vehicle. By his side was a formally dressed driver, his livery black with the same gold trim. It was a scene out of a fairytale.

"Incredible!"

Doug smiled and helped Rebecca into the carriage. "I tried to get something that looked like Cinderella's coach, but this was the best I could do."

For her part, Rebecca found the elegant open carriage preferable to Cinderella's pumpkin-turned-coach. Cinderella hadn't been able to enjoy the Texas air on her way to the ball. "It's perfect." Rebecca stroked the upholstery. The velvet was as soft as it had appeared. "The carriage is perfect, and so are these." She gestured toward the carnations that had been tinted a soft blue to complement her gown. It was almost as if Doug knew that she had planned to savor memories of this evening and had tried to create as many as possible.

He settled back as the carriage began to move, then stretched his arm out and drew Rebecca closer to him. She probably should have protested. She probably should have pulled away. Instead, Rebecca nestled in the shelter of Doug's arm, feeling protected and cherished and more than a little as if she were the heroine of one of those fairytales she'd always loved.

"Won't you tell me where we're going?"

Doug laughed and pulled her even closer. "What part of *surprise* don't you understand?"

Rebecca batted her eyelashes. "I thought maybe we could redefine the word, the way you did 'blind date.' "

"Nice try, but it's not going to work. Now, just sit back and relax."

She did. The countryside was lovely and the carriage was perfect. And her companion . . . Rebecca sighed. "I can't remember the last time I felt so relaxed." The truth was, she could. It had been the week she'd been in Hawaii with Doug. They were half a world away. Everything had changed, and yet at this moment in time it seemed nothing had changed. Once again, Rebecca felt as if she were in a dream, a dream where everyone lived happily ever after.

When the carriage turned into a drive marked by a discreet sign on the stone pillars, she gasped. "Oh, Doug!"

"Is something wrong? I heard this was a good restaurant."

That was an understatement. "It's considered the best in the Hill Country."

"After Bluebonnet Spring, that is."

Though Rebecca appreciated his loyalty, she knew there was no way her country inn could compare to this establishment. Since the restaurant was reputed to be fully booked months in advance, she couldn't imagine how Doug had managed to get a reservation on only a day's notice.

"The chef has won dozens of awards, and guests come from just about everywhere. There's even a landing pad, so that movie stars can arrive in their private planes."

"And a drive so that Rebecca Barton can arrive in her private horse-drawn carriage." Doug helped her out of that carriage, then kept her hand clasped in his as they walked to the entrance.

The restaurant was as beautiful as Rebecca had heard. Although more formal than the Bradford resort in Hawaii, it had the same attention to detail, with the linens, the china, and even the candles chosen to coordinate with the carpet and wallpaper. The décor interested Rebecca, but it was the menu she found most intriguing. Building on the Hill Country's German heritage, it featured German cuisine with uniquely Texas touches. The wiener schnitzel came with a mild jalapeno sauce, and the iced tea was peach flavored, in tribute to one of the local crops.

Three hours and five courses later, Rebecca groaned with pleasure. "I may not eat again for a week," she said as she and Doug assured the maitre d' that everything had been perfect. "I shouldn't have done it, but I couldn't resist those pastries." And, at Doug's urging, she had split two different ones with him. It wasn't simply that the desserts had appeared delicious. It was also that Rebecca didn't want the meal—or the evening—to end. Perfection like this was rare, and she wanted to enjoy it as long as she could.

Doug smiled as he signed the credit card receipt. "I have just the solution for overeating. Would Madame like to dance her dinner away?"

Rebecca looked around. "I didn't know they had dancing here."

"They don't, but this isn't the only place in Texas." Doug pulled out her chair, then led her back to the carriage, nodding at the driver's unspoken question. The coachman flicked the reins, and the steady clip-clop resumed. Ten minutes later, they stopped in front of a rough hewn wooden cabin that looked as if it catered to jeans-clad patrons.

Rebecca glanced at Doug's suit and tie and her own long gown and flowers. "I suspect we'll be a bit overdressed."

"I can promise you that no one will mind," Doug assured her as he helped her out of the carriage. When they entered the building and were greeted by the owner, the reason for Doug's promise was evident. There were no other patrons.

"Where is everyone?" The small orchestra that occupied one corner looked up when she and Doug came in and began to tune their instruments. With its highly polished dance floor surrounded by small tables, it was obvious that this establishment was designed for dancing. What wasn't obvious was who was going to do that dancing. Only the table where she and Doug sat had napkins and coasters.

Doug's answer was simple. "This is a private party."

Rebecca took a deep breath, then exhaled slowly. The man certainly knew how to make an impression. Flowers, a carriage, a gourmet dinner, and now this. "I feel so special," she said softly.

"That was the idea."

As the music began, he drew her into his arms. For the

next few hours, they danced everything from the latest fad to ballroom classics like the fox trot and the waltz. And when Rebecca knew she could dance no more, Doug nodded to the conductor.

"One last dance," he said as the opening strains of "Stranger in Paradise" filled the room. She moved into his arms and didn't protest when he lowered his head so that his cheek touched hers. This was what she thought of as their song. It was right that they were dancing cheek to cheek to this particular melody.

When the music ended someone, perhaps the owner, dimmed the lights for an instant, almost as if Rebecca and Doug were actors and this was their curtain call. Another memory for her book.

"I don't think I've ever had such a wonderful evening," Rebecca said as they rode back to Kerrville. The road was practically deserted, the only sounds the gentle clip-clop of the horse's hooves and the chirp of nocturnal insects. It was a perfect night, the air sweet with fresh grass, and the moon the smallest of crescents, not overpowering the stars. Leaning back, Rebecca gazed at the sky, enjoying the sight of the heavens, the feeling of Doug's arm around her shoulders and the scent of his after-shave blending with her flowers.

"The evening isn't over yet," Doug told her. "The carriage hasn't turned into a pumpkin."

Though it never did, Rebecca felt a pang of regret when Doug helped her out of it for the final time. There would never again be a night like this. But as he lowered the top to his car, Rebecca's spirits rose again. It might not be a carriage, but a convertible with its top down was special too.

She wasn't sure whether it was the feeling of the wind in her hair or the sound of music from her teenage years playing on the radio. Whatever the cause, Rebecca felt young and carefree. This was even better than the trip to the zoo, because tonight she had no responsibilities. There were no children in the back seat needing to be entertained. For a few minutes, nothing mattered but the fact that she and Doug were driving along a winding road, going home together, creating another memory for her to cherish.

When they arrived at Bluebonnet Spring, Doug switched off the car, then with a gallantry she thought had disappeared along with her grandparents' generation, he opened her door, helping her out. There was no reason why he needed to continue holding her hand. She could walk to her front porch unaided. But she didn't pull away from him, and so they walked hand in hand, climbing the stairs together as if they'd done it a hundred times.

Doug stopped at the door and turned to face Rebecca. "As I recall, there's a traditional way to end a date." Her breath caught as she realized what he was suggesting, and she stared at his mouth, bemused by the sight of his lips and the thought of having them pressed against hers.

As if he could read her thoughts, Doug smiled at her, and then slowly, ever so slowly, he wrapped his arms around her. Deliberately, he lowered his lips to hers. It was everything she had dreamed of and more. His lips were warm and sweet, tasting of peaches and cream and Doug. His arms were firm, sending shivers of delight down her spine.

Rebecca reached up, twining her arms around his neck, pulling him even closer. It had been wonderful dancing with him and riding in that beautiful carriage with his arm around her. She would never forget the drive home, the combination of the wind and Doug's company chasing all her worries away, or the simple act of climbing the porch steps with him. Those had been special—very, very special—but nothing compared to this. Not even the kiss they had shared in Hawaii, the one that had haunted her dreams for months, had felt like this. Nothing in her life had ever felt so good. If only it would never end.

End. With one word the spell was broken, and reality came crashing back. "No!" Wrenching herself from Doug's embrace, Rebecca stared at the man who— despite her best intentions—was a vital part of her life and her dreams. "I'm sorry, Doug," she said in a voice that quavered with emotion. "I shouldn't have let that happen." Without giving him a chance to reply, she opened the door and ran up the stairs.

He waited until he knew that Rebecca was occupied with the children before he approached her sister. "Could I convince you to go for a short drive with me?" he asked when he found Rachel in the kitchen, peeling carrots. She was his last resort. Though he had tried to make sense of the previous evening, Doug felt as if he were trying to solve an equation with far too many variables. Perhaps Rachel could help him. As her sister, she probably knew Rebecca better than anyone on earth. He was counting on the fact that she did. After last night, Doug was convinced that he knew nothing—absolutely nothing—about women in general and Rebecca specifically.

"Any particular destination?" Rachel asked, giving the vegetables a wry look.

"Any place where we won't be overheard."

Rachel nodded. "I see." She wiped her hands, then scribbled a note to Rebecca on the blackboard.

A few minutes later, Doug parked the car near a small park in the next town and opened the door for Rachel. This was one conversation he did not want to have while he was driving. He needed all his wits about him when he talked to Rebecca's sister.

"Let me guess," Rachel said as they walked to one of

the benches. "This has something to do with Cinderella."

If he hadn't been so worried, Doug might have smiled. "How did you know that that was the analogy I was going to use?"

"I heard her run up the stairs last night, and she wouldn't let me into her room. This morning she refused to even discuss your date."

Doug nodded. "If she had left a shoe behind, I would have said she was playing a game." He explained to Rachel how he'd hired the carriage, telling Rebecca he had wanted to give her Cinderella's coach. "There wasn't any shoe, though, and it didn't feel like a game." Far from it. When Rebecca had disappeared, he'd felt as if he'd lost something far more important than any game. He'd lost his chance at happiness. "I don't understand what happened. I thought she enjoyed the evening."

Two mothers pushing baby carriages walked by them. Rachel was silent for a moment, her eyes following the other women. When she spoke, her words surprised Doug. "I'm sure Rebecca did enjoy the evening. That's the problem."

How foolish he had been. He had thought Rachel would unravel the mystery. Instead, she was making it even more tangled. "Do you want to try that again, maybe in English next time?" Rachel had used words, English words, but they made no sense.

"Rebecca's afraid."

That made as little sense as Rachel's earlier statement. "Of me? I've been accused of many things, but terrorizing the women I date isn't one of them."

A quartet of elderly men entered the park, their heated discussion of the previous night's poker game effectively breaking Doug's concentration. Perhaps he and Rachel should have remained in the car.

When the men were far enough away that Doug could no longer distinguish their words, Rachel spoke. "To understand what happened, you need to know my sister's past."

He thought he did. "I know she's a widow."

As Rachel nodded, those blue eyes so like Rebecca's clouded with pain. "Did she tell you how Tim died?"

"No."

Rachel faced Doug, her gaze meeting his. "There's no easy way to say this, especially to you." She paused for a second, then said, "Tim had a heart attack. No symptoms. No warning. He went to work one day and never came home."

Doug blanched, remembering his own close call and how the surgeon had told him he'd been fortunate. He had. "That's tough."

Nodding, Rachel said, "That's only part of the story. If I know Rebecca, she didn't tell you about Danny, either." Without waiting for his reply, Rachel asked, "Did you know he had to have heart surgery?"

A shiver of pure horror swept over Doug. Danny? Loveable little Danny had undergone major surgery? "I had no idea. Danny mentioned being in the hospital when Doxy had puppies, but I thought it was to have his tonsils out or something like that."

"It was a bit more serious than that. Danny's heart was so weak that he almost died. In fact, they were afraid he wouldn't be strong enough for them to operate." Tears filled Rachel's eyes. "The surgery was as close to a miracle as I've ever experienced. For a few months after that, Rebecca's life seemed perfect. She was expecting Laura and was looking forward to a healthy baby. Then Tim died, and everything shattered. If it hadn't been for Danny, I don't know what she would have done."

Doug was speechless. What could you say when confronted with a tragedy like that?

Rachel laid her hand on his arm. "There's more. After the funeral, Rebecca told me she would never again let herself get close to a man with a weak heart."

And here Doug was, Rebecca's worst nightmare.

Chapter Ten

At last it was evening, and Rebecca could relax. She had bathed the children, read them stories, and listened until she was certain they were asleep. Now was her time. She was back in her room, the part of the inn that she considered her private refuge, and she would not—she absolutely would not—think about where she had been only twenty-four hours earlier, what she had been doing, and with whom she had been doing it. Indeed not! She was a grown woman with willpower. She could control her thoughts. Of course she could.

But, it appeared, she could not control her sister. Though she had pleaded a headache, telling Rachel what she needed was an early bedtime, here was that very same younger sister, entering Rebecca's room without so much as a knock.

"I brought some herbal tea," Rachel said as she laid the tray on the table next to Rebecca. As usual, Rachel looked as if she'd stepped out of a fashion magazine. Rebecca gave her pajamas a rueful glance. Compared to her sister's designer jeans and shirt, her comfortable attire appeared downright shabby.

"Chamomile," Rachel said. "Remember how that was Grandma Laura's favorite remedy?"

Rebecca blinked in surprise. How things had changed if Rachel was quoting the woman who had raised them! Rachel and their grandmother had had, at best, a difficult relationship, with Rachel rejecting every suggestion Grandma Laura had ever made.

"It'll cure your headache," Rachel said, again quoting their grandmother. But the next words were pure Rachel. "If you really have a headache, that is." Her expression made it clear that she doubted that.

There was no point in denying the truth. "I just needed some time alone," Rebecca admitted. Time that she obviously was not going to get.

Ignoring the broad hint, Rachel poured two cups of the steaming beverage, then handed Rebecca one. "You can't run away forever," she said, her voice as matter of fact as if she were reciting multiplication tables, not accusing her sister of cowardice.

"I'm not running away." Seeking refuge was not running away.

Rachel spooned sugar into her tea and began to stir it. "You could have fooled me." She raised her eyes to meet Rebecca's. "It was evident to anyone with even the worst observational skills that you were avoiding Doug all day. If that wasn't enough, every time I tried to talk to you, you found an excuse to do something else."

Rather than deny the accusations, which held more truth than Rebecca chose to admit, she took a sip of tea. When she had swallowed it, she said mildly, "There's a lot to do, running an inn."

"Of course there is," Rachel agreed, "but not *that* much. I've known you my whole life, and I've never seen you like this. You can claim it's something else, but it looks to me as if you're running away." Apparently taking

Rebecca's silence for assent, her sister continued, "If I were a betting woman, I'd wager that whatever it is, it's more serious than your date with Doug."

Rebecca knew when she'd met defeat. Rachel was right. There was no point in denying something that was obvious to both of them. "I had a wonderful evening with him," she said softly, her lips curving at the memory of the magical time she had shared with Doug. "It was like a movie or a book. Complete, absolute perfection. Doug had thought of every detail. He even got a horse-drawn carriage that looked like something out of a fairytale." Rebecca closed her eyes, remembering. When she opened them, she found her sister staring at her, an unfathomable expression on her face. Normally Rachel had an answer for everything. Tonight she seemed content to listen.

"I didn't want the evening to end," Rebecca continued. "It was so perfect that I hoped it would last forever. But when Doug kissed me, everything changed. I realized it wasn't just the evening I didn't want to end. I didn't want to think about him leaving when the month was over, because I didn't want our time together to ever end."

Rachel was silent for a long moment. Then she nodded slowly, her expression serious. "You love him." It was a statement, not a question.

Wrapping her arms around herself, Rebecca tried to stop the trembling that had begun to wrack her body. "I love him so much that it scares me." She looked at Rachel, willing her sister to understand. "I've never felt this way about anyone, not even Tim."

"And that bothers you." Again, it was a statement, not a question.

"Very much. I feel as if I'm being disloyal to Tim. I loved him dearly, and it seems wrong that I could love someone else even more than Tim."

"Maybe it's not more," Rachel suggested. "Just different." She poured another cup of tea and forced it into Rebecca's hand. Only when Rebecca had taken a sip did Rachel speak again. "You and Tim were practically kids when you fell in love," she said. "You're an adult now. That's why love is different." Rachel hummed the theme song from the old movie, *The Second Time Around*.

Rebecca shook her head, dismissing the thought that love was wasted on the young or that it was sweeter the second time. "Those aren't the differences," she told her sister. "The difference is that now I know there's no such thing as happily ever after."

Rachel had been leaning back in her chair. When she heard Rebecca's words, she straightened her spine and shook her head. "You're right about a lot of things, Rebecca, but you're wrong about that."

Rebecca's hand trembled so much that the tea sloshed out of the cup. She placed it back on the saucer and faced her sister. "It's easy for you to believe in happily ever after. You didn't lose your husband." Though Rachel had stayed with her during those first days when Rebecca had felt as if she were trapped in an endless nightmare, Rachel had lost a brother-in-law, not a spouse.

Rachel reached for Rebecca's hand and clasped it between both of hers. "That's true. I can only imagine how horrible it must have been for you. But you can't let that pain keep you from living."

Rebecca tried to tell herself that her sister meant well. Still, she bristled at Rachel's words. "I'm living." What would Rachel call this? Rebecca had turned a dream into reality, opening an inn and giving her children a healthy, happy home in the country. "I'm living," she replied.

"Are you?" An arched brow conveyed Rachel's skepticism even more than the tone of her voice. "It seems to me that a life without love is just existence. In my book, there's a big difference between them." She tightened her grip on Rebecca's hand as if to emphasize her words. "I imagine your life now is a lot like mine was before Grandma's will forced me back to Canela." Rachel's eyes darkened. "I thought I was happy, but now I know that I was merely putting in time. I didn't know any better. I'd never been in love, so I had nothing for comparison. But you've been in love. You know what you're missing. That's why I can't imagine why you're throwing away a chance at happiness."

Rachel didn't understand. Perhaps no one could. "You're making a rather rash assumption, Rachel. You assume I have something to throw away. You assume someone's offered me a chance at happiness. The fact is, Doug will be going home soon." Rebecca wouldn't, she absolutely would not, count the days and hours that were left. "Doug's life is in Detroit; mine is here. The most important thing in his life is his company. You know nothing is more important to me than my children." Rebecca shook her head slowly, trying to ignore the sadness that welled up inside her. "The simple fact is, Doug and I have no future together. We never did. That's why it was foolish of me to fall in love." To Rebecca's dismay, her voice broke as she uttered the last words.

Rachel stroked Rebecca's hands in a gesture Rebecca remembered their grandmother using. "Love is never foolish," Rachel said, her voice filled with emotion. "If there's one thing I've learned, it's that love is the most important part of life. Don't give up on it, Rebecca. You don't have to wait for it to be offered. Go after it."

If only it were that simple! Tears welled in Rebecca's eyes as she spoke. "I'm not that brave. I can't risk loving a man who might be taken from me the next day." She had gone through that once, and it was worse than anything Rebecca could imagine, short of losing one of her children.

"What about your children?" Rachel asked softly. "When Tim died, you told me one of the things that hurt the most was knowing they would grow up without their father. Don't they deserve a stepfather?"

Rebecca couldn't count the sleepless nights she'd spent worrying about Danny and Laura growing up without a father. Since Doug had come to Bluebonnet Spring, her worries had changed. Now she feared that they'd become so attached to Doug that they'd be devastated when he left. How much worse it would be if Doug became a part of their life and then was taken from them the way Tim had been. Rebecca could not expose her children to that kind of loss. There was, however, another solution. "They'll have a father if I marry Jim."

Her sister raised both eyebrows. "Jim, the guy who's always hanging around here?" The tone of her voice left no doubt of her opinion.

"That's not exactly the way I'd describe him." Rebecca glared at her sister. "He's Jim, the man who'll be a good father to my children."

And if he didn't set her heart on fire, well . . . maybe that was for the best. A heart that wasn't engaged couldn't be broken.

It wasn't the most beautiful of mornings. Far from it. The sun was hiding behind a shroud of thick clouds, and the previous day's breeze had dissipated, leaving the air heavy with the promise of rain. The only way to describe the weather was dismal—the same word that Doug would use to describe his mood. Even though he understood the reason why, he didn't like the fact that Rebecca was avoiding him. He didn't like it at all.

Rebecca was the most wonderful woman he'd ever met. She was pretty, and witty, and fun to be with. Unfortunately, she also fled from him as if he had the Bubonic plague, when all he had was a heart that the doctor assured him would soon be almost as good as new. Doug knew that "almost" wasn't good enough for Rebecca. He clenched his fists, then relaxed each finger individually. It wasn't fair, but if there was one thing he had learned, it was that life wasn't always fair.

He was a man who was accustomed to solving problems. Companies paid him a lot of money to do exactly that, but this time the problem was one he couldn't solve. Doug couldn't tell Rebecca there was nothing wrong with his heart, even though his physician had assured him that with proper diet and exercise, he would probably never have another attack. "Probably" wasn't good enough for Rebecca, just as "almost" wasn't. And so she shunned him.

Her children did not. To the contrary, for the past two days, they had clung to Doug, almost as if they sensed something was wrong and were trying to compensate for their mother's distance. Even when Rebecca tried to redirect their attention, Danny and Laura begged Doug to play with them. Which was why he was sitting on the edge of the sandbox, patting a brown dachshund and directing castle construction.

"Watch me, Doug." Danny tugged on his arm. "I make a ter . . . toor . . . What did you call it?" The little boy struggled with the word.

"A turret." Doug couldn't help smiling at Danny's attempt to embellish the castle. The tower was lopsided and top-heavy, leading to very predictable sagging, which would lead to eventual collapse. "Let's try it this way." Doug settled Doxy with a rawhide bone, then showed Danny how to shape a tower.

"Me, me!" Laura, who'd been playing peacefully in the

far corner of the sandbox, picked up a fistful of sand and approached the turret, obviously planning to help in the construction.

Hoping to avert the impending disaster, Doug pointed to the space in front of the castle. "Let's work on the moat." Matching his actions to his words, he started to dig a trench. Laura watched him for a second, then began to dig, spraying sand as vigorously as Doxy when she was burying a bone. A minute later, Laura stopped, flung her arms around Doug's neck, and kissed him.

Though he'd been deeply engrossed in his tower, the loud smacking caused Danny to raise his head. He stared at his sister for a second, then announced, "Laura likes you."

The warmth that swept through Doug was like nothing he'd experienced. "I like her. You too, pardner."

Apparently satisfied by the response, Danny grinned and started to build a second turret, leaving Doug to wonder why the affection of two small children brought him more pleasure than the approval of his board of directors and why watching a boy construct a sandcastle seemed as exciting as designing Apex's new filters.

When the turret was half done, Danny turned toward Doug, a frown creasing his forehead.

"Problem, pardner?"

Danny nodded. "Mom says you're gonna leave."

The tone of his voice and the puzzled expression on Laura's face tugged on Doug's heartstrings. Even though he knew it was both inevitable and necessary, leaving was something he didn't want to think about, much less discuss with a child. "I've got a business to run in Detroit," Doug said as evenly as he could.

"Where's that?"

"Far away." In more ways than one. Though it was only a few hours away on an airplane, the hectic pace at Apex was a world apart from the tranquility of Bluebonnet Spring.

Danny wrinkled his nose, obviously trying to understand. "Even further than Canela?" he asked.

"I'm afraid so."

The boy's frown deepened. "Me and Laura wish you didn't have to go."

"Me too." Who would have thought that Doug West, the man who had rebuilt companies, would enjoy sitting in a pile of sand building a simple castle with turrets that leaned more precariously than the tower of Pisa? Who would have thought that the man who wheeled and dealed with the best would find himself challenged by two young children? And who could have predicted that he'd become attached to those children and their all too attractive mother?

Who'd have thought it?

Rebecca poured soap into the dispenser and closed the dishwasher door. Another day was almost over. Another day without talking to Doug about what had happened That Night. That was how she thought of it, as a special occasion that deserved capital letters. It had been special, and Doug deserved an explanation for the way she'd run away and the way she was avoiding him. But putting emotions into words wasn't easy, especially these emotions.

Rachel could say all she wanted to about seizing the opportunity, but there was, Rebecca had discovered, a big difference between planning to do something and actually doing it. She hadn't been ready yesterday; she wasn't ready today. As for tomorrow . . . Rebecca wasn't sure she'd ever be ready to talk to Doug. Instead she got through each day as best she could and tried not to think about the fact that each day brought her closer to the one when Doug would leave Bluebonnet Spring.

"Rebecca."

Startled, she turned toward the door. "Hello, Jim." She hadn't expected him tonight. More than anyone she knew, Jim was a man of routine. This was one of the nights when he had other activities. Had his buddies cancelled bowling? And why was he wearing a new shirt?

Jim leaned against the doorway, his posture apparently casual, although both hands were fisted. "The moon is pretty tonight," he said. "I thought we might go for a walk."

Rebecca tried not to let her surprise show. Though she had known Jim for close to a year, she had never heard him discuss the moon. He wasn't the kind of man who engaged in casual discussions of the weather, and he certainly didn't speculate on the beauty of celestial bodies. He didn't even like to walk. Cars were meant for transportation and horses for recreation, he had once declared. Walking was for those who had neither cars nor horses. But tonight, it appeared, was a night for change.

"Sure," Rebecca said, although a knot began to form in the pit of her stomach. The tone of Jim's voice and the way he looked at the floor rather than meet her gaze made her suspect that Jim had more in mind than stargazing. She shouldn't have been surprised, and she wasn't—not really. She and Jim had been moving toward this moment since the day they'd met. And yet now that it was here, all she felt was apprehension. "I'll ask Rachel to watch the children."

Only minutes later, they were outside, strolling toward the pond that gave Bluebonnet Spring its name. Though Jim tried to make casual conversation, it was obvious that he was nervous. She hadn't been mistaken about his intentions. The knot in Rebecca's stomach began to grow.

When they reached the far end of the pond, Jim stopped. He turned so that he was facing Rebecca, and in the moonlight, she could see beads of perspiration on his forehead, despite the fact that it was a cool night. Had Tim been this nervous? Rebecca didn't think so.

Jim cleared his throat, started to speak, then cleared it again. "Rebecca," he said at last, "I think you know how much I care for you and your children."

She swallowed deeply, trying to dislodge the knot that seemed to have filled her stomach and was making its way into her throat.

"The brightest moments of my day are the ones I spend here with you." Jim's voice was earnest. "If I had my way, I'd never leave." He dropped to one knee, and pulling a box from his pocket, extended it to her. There was no question of what the velvet cube contained. Only one piece of jewelry was packaged in a box that size and shape. "Rebecca, will you do me the honor of becoming my wife?"

She swallowed again. This was the moment she had anticipated, the question she had known he was going to ask. She had considered it carefully and she knew what she would answer. She would say "yes." That was the answer Jim expected. That was the answer everyone expected. Most importantly, it was the right decision for Danny and Laura. Jim would be the father they needed. Rebecca opened her mouth.

"I'm sorry, Jim." The words flowed, seemingly of their own volition. "I can't."

"What?" He leaped to his feet, thrusting the velvet box back into his pocket. "I thought you cared for me." The bewilderment in Jim's voice wrenched Rebecca's heart. He was a good man and a kind one. Though he deserved only goodness and kindness in return, she had hurt him.

"I do care for you." She wouldn't say she loved him, for he would misunderstand. "You're a wonderful friend. I care for you as a friend." That was what her heart had known; that was the reason she couldn't accept Jim's proposal, even though logic said he would be a good husband and father. "That's not enough." Rebecca had been married, and she knew that marriage was more than friendship. "You deserve more than I can give you, Jim. You deserve a woman who loves you."

As the moonlight revealed deep furrows between Jim's eyes, Rebecca's heart ached at the thought that she had put them there. "I have enough love for both of us," he declared.

Remembering how Rachel had sought to comfort her, Rebecca stretched out her hand and clasped Jim's. "Marriage doesn't work that way. There has to be love on both sides if it's going to be a true marriage." She squeezed his hand. "I'm sorry, Jim. I wish I could have given you a different answer." If only her heart hadn't overruled her mind!

Jim tugged his hand free and took a step backward, as if he couldn't bear to be near her. "It's Doug West, isn't it? You're going to marry him." Jim spat the words at Rebecca. "I knew that man should never have come here. Women can't resist playing nurse."

If only Jim knew how wrong he was! "The problem isn't Doug," Rebecca said as calmly as she could. "The problem is me. I can't turn friendship into love." But, oh, how she wished she could.

Chapter Eleven

B*rring. Brring.* Doug blinked in surprise as he realized that the sound was his cell phone ringing. He was back in his room after breakfast, changing into what he'd come to think of as his sandbox clothes. He unfolded the receiver, his pulse accelerating with the realization that the call must be important. When Doug had boarded the plane for San Antonio, Terri had given him a new phone with a number no one knew and had been vigilant about protecting his privacy. Not only had she refused to give the number to the rest of his staff, but she had never called him. The phone, she had insisted, was his security blanket. He could use it for outgoing calls, but no one at Apex would bother him. If anyone at the office wanted to reach Doug, they would leave a message via email or on his office voice mail. Doug wasn't sure why he kept the cell phone turned on, other than habit.

"What's up?" Recognizing Terri's number on the caller ID, he dispensed with polite greetings.

"Greg's panicked." Though Terri kept her voice low and even, Doug could hear the tension in it. "A whole shipment of fiber is bad, and no one's got any in stock."

This was bad news, no doubt about it. "Greg can't figure out how we're going to deliver the HPX filters on time."

Groaning, Doug had a fleeting wish that he hadn't kept the phone on. "I get the picture. Why don't you transfer me to Greg?" He heard Terri's sigh of relief in the second before she pressed the transfer button.

Four hours later, Doug leaned back in his chair. The desk in front of him held two empty coffee pots, a mug, and a plate that had once carried sandwiches. Doug wasn't sure whether Rebecca had heard the phone ringing or whether she simply guessed how serious the situation was from the look on his face when she'd come in to check the room, but within minutes the first pot of coffee had arrived. She had said nothing, obviously not wanting to interrupt the series of telecons that had formed his day, but Rebecca had seemed attuned to his needs, bringing nourishment before he realized he needed it. She had even brought him another memo pad just seconds before he used the last sheet of his. The woman was incredible!

Doug closed his eyes and propped his feet on the desk. He'd done it. Working with Greg and the rest of the team, Doug had called in favors from suppliers, managing to locate the raw materials they needed. Their production line wouldn't stop, and they'd be able to meet their commitments to their customers. The problem was solved, everyone at Apex was elated, and he was tired.

Doug's eyes flew open as he realized that fatigue was the only thing he felt. There was none of the adrenaline rush that normally accompanied crisis resolution. There was no sense of exhilaration, not even a modicum of satisfaction. All he felt was tired. And that wasn't normal. When he'd resolved the last HPX emergency by persuading the union to allow its members to work long hours, Doug had felt a basic level of accomplishment. Not today. Today he felt drained.

He was glad that he'd been able to solve the problem, but that was primarily because it meant that he could spend the afternoon with Danny and Laura. As he'd worked through the morning, Doug had felt a rising sense of annoyance each time he'd glanced at his watch and wondered whether the children were constructing the outer bailey wall. What on earth was happening to him that he cared more about building sandcastles than running his company?

Doug closed his eyes again, not wanting to look at the pile of crumpled paper. At one point when a supplier had put him on extended hold, Doug had resorted to making and flying paper airplanes. He hadn't done that since high school.

Other people might complain about their jobs, but Doug had always loved his. Though he hadn't liked it when Lisa had broken their engagement, telling him that he loved the company more than he did her, Doug couldn't deny that she was right. He had cared more about Apex than the woman he had almost married. That was one of the reasons why the broken engagement hadn't hurt much more than his pride.

Lisa had claimed that Doug lived to work, and the assessment had been accurate. But now . . . now he felt as if there was a distance between him and Apex, a distance that had nothing to do with the physical miles that separated him from his office. Today, when he'd been working with Greg and the others, he'd felt almost as if it were someone else's company whose future had been at stake, and that he'd been a consultant, brought in to help solve the problems. Instead of being deeply involved, he had felt detached, and the problem had seemed almost empirical. What on earth was happening?

A month ago he couldn't imagine anything other than doing what he'd always done, working ridiculous hours to ensure that the company was successful. And now . . .

now it was difficult to imagine returning to that life. Now, though he knew he wanted something different, the identity of that something eluded him.

Doug lowered his feet to the floor, pushed the chair back and strode to the window. Looking down, he saw Rebecca walking slowly through the garden, Danny on one side, Laura on the other, each gripping her hand. Today she was wearing one of the long, flowing dresses she seemed to like, and even though the sun was still hidden, a large-brimmed hat. Occasionally she'd bend down to sniff a flower, and the children would take turns smelling the same blossom. It was an ordinary scene, one that Doug imagined was repeated across the country dozens of times a day. And yet it didn't seem ordinary. As he watched them, a shaft of longing pierced Doug. The scene before him was beautiful, but it was incomplete. It needed a man, and oh! how he wanted to be that man.

Memories of the day he'd taken Rebecca and her children to the zoo rushed through him, startling him with their intensity. Even before the older couple had referred to the four of them as a family, Doug had known there was something special about that day. That was why, at the oddest times, he'd remember Danny spilling ketchup or Laura clinging to him. No matter the memory, it was always accompanied by Rebecca's smile.

At the time, Doug hadn't realized what was happening, but now he recognized the day for what it was: a turning point. That was the day the direction of his life began to change. There had been a time when what Doug had wanted from life was success in the business world. More money, a larger staff, a better title. Now he wanted a family. And not just any family. He wanted this one.

Doug turned away from the window and tried to slow his breathing. It was so simple. Why hadn't he seen it before? He loved Rebecca. He'd known that he enjoyed her company and that he couldn't stop thinking of her. He'd known that he wanted to erase every bit of unhappiness from her life. He'd known that the idea of leaving her had bothered him. He'd known all that, but he hadn't put the pieces together. Now it was clear. He loved Rebecca, and his love for her was the most important thing in his life. Everything else paled next to it. That was why he felt this way. That was why this morning's work hadn't felt fulfilling.

He loved Rebecca! The thought was so exciting that Doug wanted to shout it from the rooftops. He wanted to take out a full page ad in *The New York Times,* proclaiming his love. He wanted to hire one of those planes that dragged banners behind them. But he couldn't do any of those things. Not yet. There were problems he had to resolve first.

Doug knew that Jim Locke wanted to marry Rebecca. Perhaps she had already agreed to be his wife. If so, Doug would have to convince her to break her engagement. Once that hurdle was crossed, there was the matter of Doug's health. He knew she was skittish. Oh, why mince words? Rebecca wasn't skittish where his health was concerned, she was petrified. Still, there had to be a way to convince her that the risk was minimal and that love was worth that risk. It wouldn't be easy. Doug knew that. He would have to find a way to persuade Rebecca, but if there was one thing he was good at, it was persuading people. He would succeed. He had to.

As he descended the stairs, Doug heard a soft humming in the parlor. Excellent. There was only one person at Bluebonnet Spring who hummed. The humming meant that Rachel was indoors. If he was to succeed, Doug needed an ally. Rachel would be a good one. He entered the parlor.

Rachel glanced up from the book she'd been reading,

her eyes narrowing as she studied Doug. "You look more relaxed than I've seen you. Did something happen?"

Doug tried not to cringe at the woman's perceptiveness. He hadn't realized his feelings were so obvious. Yes, indeed, something had happened, but Doug had no intention of telling Rachel everything. "I realized I could retire," he said truthfully. That was the least important realization he'd reached, but—if everything went the way he hoped—it would enable him to turn his dreams into reality.

Rachel raised a skeptical eyebrow. "Aren't you a bit young? Besides, I heard you were a . . ." She hesitated, obviously reluctant to pronounce the word.

"A workaholic?" Doug finished the sentence for her as he took the chair across from her.

"Well . . . um . . . yes."

"Guilty on both counts." There was no reason to deny the obvious. "There's nothing I can do about my age, but I plan to change the second part." Doug had never minded being labeled a workaholic until today, when he'd realized there was a price to pay for making work his whole life.

He flashed Rebecca's sister what he hoped was a persuasive smile. "I realized that I can work a lot less and still be satisfied." Because there would be other things—much more important things—to occupy his day. Things like a small boy and his sister. Things like their mother. "If I want to keep my fingers in the corporate pies, I can do what a lot of other executives do. I can arrange a few consulting gigs and join the speech circuit."

Slowly and deliberately Rachel laid the book on the table next to her. "Where would your home be?" Though her tone was neutral, the way she kept her eyes focused on his face told Doug she was more than a little interested in his answer. He had the oddest feeling that he was a suitor, asking his prospective father-in-law for permission to court his daughter. Though he wasn't asking Rachel for permission, Doug did want her approval or at least her cooperation.

"That depends." *On your sister.*

She nodded slowly. "I see." And, though she said nothing more, Doug suspected that Rachel had somehow heard his unspoken words. "I don't want to betray any confidences, and I won't," she added, "but Jim came to see my sister last night."

That was news to Doug. Unwelcome news, if the reason for the visit was the one he thought. Doug frowned, trying to remember whether Rebecca had been wearing a new ring this morning. She might have been. Doug wouldn't claim to be the most observant of men, and this morning he'd been preoccupied. He raised an eyebrow, encouraging Rebecca's sister to continue.

Rachel kept her expression impassive. "I don't know what they said, but judging from the way he slammed his car door when he left, I don't think their conversation went the way Jim expected."

Elation surged through Doug with the force of a runaway train. If he had interpreted Rachel's words correctly, Rebecca hadn't agreed to marry Jim. Wonderful! Doug wouldn't have to persuade her to break her engagement. One barrier down, one to go. "I see," he said, deliberately keeping his voice as neutral as Rachel's. "I might need your help."

This time Rachel couldn't hide her curiosity. Her eyes sparkled and she leaned forward as she asked, "What do you mean?"

"It can't have escaped your observation that Rebecca treats me as if I had the plague."

Rachel nodded. "I might not have phrased it exactly that way, but I can't disagree with you. How can I help?"

Doug leaned forward. "Here's what I want to do . . ."

* * *

"You work too hard."

Rebecca poured her sister a cup of tea, then counted to three before she said, "You're not the first person who's told me that." When Rachel had appeared in her room after the children went to sleep, bearing a pot of tea and some of the shortbread that Rebecca had carefully frozen so there would be dessert available while she was at the innkeepers' conference, Rebecca had known her sister wanted to have another of what she called their "sisterly chats." Though Rebecca wasn't anxious for an encore of Rachel urging her to declare her love to Doug, she also knew her sister well enough to realize that the simplest way to deal with her was to let her have her say. And fortunately, Rachel didn't want to discuss Doug. It was far easier to respond to accusations of workaholism than cowardice in love.

"Just because I'm not the first to say it doesn't make it any less true." Rachel settled back in the wing chair and sipped her tea. "I don't want to argue with you. I just want to take you and the children out to lunch tomorrow. You need the change of scenery, and it'll be one less meal for you to cook."

Though the idea was tempting, Rebecca shook her head. "I have to get ready for the innkeepers' conference." Among other things, she would have to replace the food Rachel had taken from the freezer.

"What a lame excuse. You know you never pack until fifteen minutes before you leave, and the conference is days away."

"Packing isn't the only thing I have to do. Besides, I can't leave the inn unattended."

"Of course you can. Tomorrow's Kate's day to work. She can answer the phone and check in any walk-ins."

"But . . ."

Rachel wagged a finger at her. "I want to do this. Please let me."

Rebecca doubted anyone in Canela had ever been able to resist her sister when she was in her persuasive mode. Rebecca certainly couldn't. "All right."

"I could have driven," Rebecca said the next morning when she and the children were seated in Rachel's SUV. Though she had assumed that they would take her van, since it already had the car seats installed, Rachel had insisted on driving.

"Of course you could have driven," her sister agreed, "but the whole point of this excursion was for you to relax. Now just enjoy your children."

"The same children who are the reason we're fifteen minutes late leaving." Laura wouldn't budge from the house without her stuffed dog, and for some reason that dog wasn't to be found in any of its normal spots. Rebecca had spent five minutes searching for it, only to discover that it had been tucked into the corner of the parlor window seat, a most unlikely location, since the children were not allowed to play in the parlor. Another five minutes had been lost, convincing Danny that Doxy could not go with them, and yet another five as they'd transferred the car seats to Rachel's vehicle. If the trip was supposed to allow her to relax, so far it had been a dismal failure.

"Fifteen minutes shouldn't be a problem," Rachel said as she slowed for a curve in the road. "The restaurant holds reservations for ten minutes. I know I can make up the time." But, though Rachel had once been known for her flagrant disregard of speed limits, today she drove at exactly the posted speed. It must be because she had the children in the back seat. Rebecca could think of no other reason for her sister's caution.

Settling back in her seat, Rebecca tried to enjoy the scenery. Though she loved her home state at any time, there was no doubt that spring was her favorite season. The burgeoning leaf buds and the fresh green of the grass filled her heart with joy. Spring was a season of promises and possibilities. Today, though, she found herself unable to relax. It was only because they might be late for lunch, she told herself. It had nothing to do with her long-term guest and the magical evening they had spent together.

"Are you sure you won't tell me where we're going?" Rebecca asked her sister. The unknown lunch destination was yet another reminder of an evening she'd rather forget. "You're being so mysterious that I think you've been spending too much time with Doug. His habits are rubbing off on you."

"Can you blame me for wanting to be with him? The man's almost as handsome as my husband."

Almost? Rebecca stared at her sister. How could she possibly think that? Though Scott wasn't bad looking, Doug was far more handsome than her brother-in-law. There was absolutely no comparison. It wasn't just that Doug was tall, dark, and handsome. He was also witty and charming and . . . "How is Scott?" Rebecca asked. She had to do something to stop herself from thinking of Doug. "How's Scott doing in the childcare contest with Luke?"

Rachel's smile said she was still as much in love with her husband as she'd been from the day she returned to Canela. "According to Scott, everything's fine. He even learned to take the lid off the baby food jar before he puts it in the microwave." Rachel chuckled, as if she considered that a major accomplishment. "I think he's enjoying this whole adventure. He's confident he'll beat Luke."

"For your sake, I hope he does." Rebecca turned and

pulled the plastic cup from Laura's hand. "Sorry, sweetie, but you can't hit your brother with that." Laura appeared to have mistaken her brother's arm for a drum.

Rachel shrugged and slowed the car as they rounded a curve. Though she glanced at her watch repeatedly, she was driving as if they had hours to spare. "It won't really bother Scott if he doesn't win. He'll just find another way to challenge Luke." Rachel braked again as they crossed a small bridge. "Scott's not a competitive man. He enjoys playing the game; winning's not as important as just playing."

Tim had been like that, which was one of the reasons he and Scott had become good friends. That easy-going attitude had also made Tim easy to live with. He hadn't been what anyone would call "high maintenance," whereas Doug . . . Rebecca frowned. It was ridiculous that everything reminded her of Doug.

As they entered a small town, Rachel glanced at her watch again. "We're almost there. Just in time." She slowed as they approached the center of the town, stopping in front of an old Victorian house that advertised itself as a tea room. Though Rebecca had heard of the restaurant, she had never eaten there. "Only nine and a half minutes late," Rachel said with satisfaction. "Time to spare."

Thirty seconds was not Rebecca's idea of an adequate safety margin. All she could hope was that the restaurant didn't actually enforce the ten minute rule. Rachel must have read her mind, for she said, "Rebecca, you'd better run inside and save our table. I'll park the car and bring the kids. We'll be there in five minutes."

Rebecca looked at her children, who were—thank goodness—in their angelic mode. "Are you sure you can handle them?" she asked her sister. When Rachel nodded, Rebecca climbed out of the car, admonishing Danny and Laura to be good for Aunt Rachel.

The inside of the tea house was as delightful as its exterior had promised. Fresh flowers adorned the hostess' stand, and the wide center hallway boasted crystal sconces and an Oriental rug. The décor was more formal than Bluebonnet Spring, making Rebecca wonder why her sister had chosen it for lunch with two young children. As she waited for the hostess, Rebecca could see four small rooms off the hallway, each with half a dozen tables, all of which were filled. There was not, however, a highchair in sight. This was definitely not a place for children.

"Reservations for Sanders," Rebecca said when the hostess returned to her station. "The rest of the party will be arriving soon."

The woman consulted the seating chart, then nodded. "If you'll follow me." She led the way along the hallway and through the back door onto a covered porch. Larger and less formal than the inside rooms, the porch boasted ten tables, only one of which was occupied. Rebecca stared. Not only was the table occupied, but it was occupied by a man she knew very well.

"Your friend is waiting," the hostess said, gesturing toward the table for two.

Rebecca stopped in mid-stride. This wasn't happening. It couldn't be. "There must be some mistake. My sister reserved a table for four with a highchair."

The hostess shook her head. "The woman who made the reservation was specific. This is what she asked for. Now, if you'll excuse me, I need to seat another guest." Her heels clicking on the stone floor, the hostess left Rebecca to her fate.

"What are you doing here?" Rebecca demanded as she approached the table.

Doug pulled out the second chair and urged Rebecca to sit. There were two place settings and two glasses of

water, but no menus. "Having lunch with you," he said
smoothly as she took the seat across from him. The man
had no right to be so handsome. Today he was wearing
khaki pants and a navy polo shirt. Hundreds of men wore
the same clothes, but they didn't look like Doug. They
didn't have the panache that turned ordinary clothing into
something special.

Annoyed at the direction her thoughts continued to
take, Rebecca clenched her teeth. "Where's Rachel going
to sit?"

"She and the children are having lunch at the Sonic,
which, your sister assured me, is their preferred dining
establishment."

A spurt of anger raced through Rebecca. It all made
sense now. No wonder Rachel hadn't hurried. She hadn't
wanted to arrive early. No wonder Laura's toy had been in
the parlor. Rachel had probably put it there, knowing that
would cause a delay. No wonder she had insisted Rebecca
come into the restaurant alone. She'd been set up by her
sister.

As she started to rise, Doug shook his head. "Look,
Rebecca, we need to talk. This was the only way I could
figure to keep you from running away."

She glared at Doug, as angry with him as she was with
her sister. The scheme was his. Rachel had simply helped
execute it. "You like to win, don't you?" Doug was a man
who could persuade, and if that didn't work, manipulate
labor unions and boards of directors until he got his way.
Apparently he thought the same tactics would work with
her. He was wrong.

"Of course I like to win, but what does that have to do
with us?"

He didn't understand. Rebecca doubted he ever would.
"It has a lot to do with us. Winning isn't everything."

The dining room was still empty, and no one had come

to give them menus. Rebecca wondered if this was like the dance hall. Had Doug arranged it so that they'd have a private room for their talk?

He nodded slowly, and for a second Rebecca thought he was answering her unspoken question. "I agree," he said, his dark eyes serious. "Winning isn't everything. It's not even the most important thing."

Rebecca blinked and took a sip of water to cover her confusion. She hadn't expected him to say that. The Doug she knew—or the Doug she thought she knew—believed that winning was everything. She took another sip, then asked, "What is the most important thing?"

"Love."

Surprise morphed into shock and for a second Rebecca was unable to speak. "Love?"

Doug nodded. "That's the reason I'm here and the reason I asked Rachel to bring you here." He reached across the table, capturing one of Rebecca's hands between both of his. His were warm and firm, and though she didn't want it to happen, they sent shivers of delight up her arms, reminding her of the night he'd kissed her. "There are things between us that we need to talk about," he said. Her face must have reflected her confusion, for he nodded again. "Yes, those things include love."

Doug swallowed, and Rebecca saw an expression cross his face. It was so fleeting that she wasn't certain, but she thought it was doubt. Whatever he was going to say, it appeared that he was unsure of her reaction. He swallowed again, then began. "Rebecca, I love you more than I ever dreamed it was possible to love a woman." Doug's voice was husky with emotion, and that combined with the words he'd spoken literally stole Rebecca's breath. No one had ever looked at her the way Doug was looking at her and no one had ever made her feel the way his declaration of love did, as if—for one moment in time—

everything was perfect and there truly was such a thing as happily ever after.

Doug tightened his grip on Rebecca's hands. "I want to marry you and help you raise Danny and Laura. And—if we're so blessed—I want to help you raise a child of our own." He took a deep breath, letting it out slowly. "Will you marry me, Rebecca?"

A lifetime ago, she would have said yes. The man who sat across from her, love shining from his eyes, was the man who could turn her days from ordinary into spectacular. He was the man her children already trusted. And, though she had tried to deny it, he was the man she loved so deeply it hurt to think of never seeing him again. A lifetime ago, she would have said yes. But that was a lifetime ago. What mattered was today. Today there was only one possible response.

"I can't." Even though she knew it was the right answer, it hurt to pronounce those words.

Doug's eyes darkened with pain, a pain Rebecca knew she'd caused. "Can you tell me that you don't love me?" he demanded, his voice harsh, his breathing ragged. When Rebecca tried to pull her hand free from his grasp, he tightened it. "I may be mistaken, but I thought you loved me."

She wouldn't lie. Even though they had no future together, Doug deserved the truth. "I do love you."

Lines formed between his eyes, and deep creases bracketed his mouth. "Then why won't you marry me?"

Rebecca closed her eyes, trying to force back the dark images, images of a policeman knocking on her door, of herself standing next to a polished wooden casket and later kneeling beside a simple gravestone, memories of Danny's endless questions about when his daddy would be home. When she regained her composure, Rebecca opened her eyes and looked at Doug. "I couldn't bear it if you . . ." Though she tried, she couldn't force herself to pronounce the final word.

"Died." He completed the sentence for her.

Rebecca nodded. "I went through that once, and I never, ever want to endure that kind of pain again. The next time would be worse for me and my children."

Doug was silent for a moment, his expression inscrutable. When he spoke, his voice was low and fervent. "I can't give you any guarantees, Rebecca. You know that. I can't promise that I'll live to be a hundred. All I can promise is that I'll love you every single day that we're given. I'll love you and Danny and Laura, and I'll do everything in my power to make you happy."

The picture he painted was a happy one. Rebecca could imagine the four of them, sitting on the porch swing after dinner. She could imagine Doug greeting guests with her, and the two of them walking around the pond, hand in hand. She could imagine all that, and yet she could not dismiss the other images, the ones of an empty chair at the table, the ones of a closet that held only her clothes, the ones of her son's tearstained face.

"I know you'd do that, but . . ."

"We'd be happy together," he said, his eyes meeting hers and willing her to agree. "I know we would."

But for how long? That was the question. That was the fear that haunted her.

"I can't do it, Doug. I can't risk that kind of pain again." For something deep inside Rebecca told her that it would be worse this time. Rachel was right. When she had fallen in love with Tim, Rebecca had been a teenager. Though she had loved him deeply, the feelings she had for Doug were stronger than the love she had had for her husband. It had been horrible losing Tim, but if she lost Doug, it would be worse for her and for Danny. And now there was Laura to consider. "I can't, Doug. I just can't."

His lips thinned, and Rebecca sensed the anger that simmered below the surface. "You're saying that because life comes without a guarantee, you're willing to throw away our chance at happiness." When Rebecca did not reply, Doug continued, "I don't understand you, Rebecca. I've always thought you were independent and courageous. Now it appears that you're a coward."

She flinched but couldn't deny the accusation. "If being a coward means avoiding heartbreak, then I guess I am one." Rachel might claim that she was existing rather than living, but Rebecca knew that what she was doing was ensuring that she and her children survived.

Doug was silent for a long moment, absorbing her words. When he spoke, his voice held a note of despair she'd never heard. "Is there anything I can say or do to change your mind?"

Rebecca shook her head. "Just take me home."

He rose, throwing a few bills on the table. "I know you're going to the innkeepers' conference on Monday," he said as they walked outside. "I'll leave Bluebonnet Spring before you return." He opened the car door and helped Rebecca inside. "I'd check out today, but I promised Danny I'd teach him to fish while you're gone, and I don't want to disappoint him."

Rebecca blinked back the tears. "You're a good man."

"I'd be a good father and a good husband," he said.

"I know." That made it even worse.

Chapter Twelve

"Would you like lunch?" A flight attendant offered Rebecca one of the plastic baskets filled with a sandwich, chips, and an apple that the airline called lunch.

Rebecca shook her head. On another day she would have accepted, but the mild indigestion that had bothered her at home hadn't disappeared, and she had no desire to eat. It was probably nothing more than stress. Heaven knew that she had had enough of that. Apparently reconsidering his decision to stay at the inn, Doug had left Bluebonnet Spring within minutes of bringing her home from the tea house. He said he would stay in a hotel in Kerrville until she left for the conference. Only then would he return to fulfill his promise to Danny. It was the day Doug had left that the indigestion had started.

Rebecca missed Doug. There was no denying that. It wasn't simply that she missed the time they had spent together. She missed everything. She missed pouring him a cup of coffee each morning. She missed the way he'd try to load the dishwasher, never seeming to remember which way the silverware was supposed to go. She missed watching him play with Danny and Laura. She even missed hearing his laptop chirp when it booted.

And it wasn't only Rebecca who missed Doug. Danny made no secret of his displeasure that his grown-up play-mate was gone. In apparent retaliation, he insisted on tak-ing Doxy everywhere with him, protesting loudly when Rebecca refused to allow the dog in the bathroom. Even Laura sulked. Neither one appeared to believe Rebecca when she told them that Doug would be back in a few days. Seeing her children's sadness wrenched Rebecca's heart, but it also confirmed her decision. If Danny and Laura had grown this attached to Doug in only a few weeks, what would it be like if she married him and he became a part of the family? How would they bear it if he were taken from them the way Tim had been? She couldn't—she wouldn't—expose her children to that kind of risk.

As the plane began to circle San Francisco International, Rebecca laid a hand on her stomach. Surely now that she was away from Bluebonnet Spring and the ever present memories of Doug, she would feel better. After all, the city by the bay was reported to be one of the most beautiful in America, as romantic as Hawaii, but in a different way.

Romantic? Where had that thought come from? She had no reason to be thinking about romance. She was a businesswoman, coming to attend a conference that would help her strengthen her inn. She was here to learn, not to dream about love and romance. But, Rebecca dis-covered after her first few hours in the city, it was difficult not to dream. The city was as beautiful as she'd heard, and the large hotel on Union Square where the conference was being held did everything imaginable to make its guests feel special.

"I can't believe they're bringing us cookies and bottled

water just because we have to stand in line." The woman ahead of Rebecca in the registration queue turned and addressed her.

Rebecca shrugged her shoulders. "Believe it or not, I did something similar when all my weekend guests decided to arrive at the same time."

"Then you ought to be leading one of the seminars," the woman, who introduced herself as Deirdre, said.

"Hardly. I'm just a beginner."

"Me too."

As they inched their way to the head of the line, the two women compared notes and discovered that not only were both their inns in Texas, but they also shared similar philosophies. By the time they received their registration packets, Rebecca and Deirdre had arranged to meet for meals and to attend different sessions to, as Deirdre put it, maximize their learning.

And learn, Rebecca did. By the time the early bird sessions were finished that evening, she had taken copious notes on topics as diverse as targeted advertising and shortening the time required for routine housekeeping.

"I never knew you could make a bed without walking around it more than once," she told Deirdre the next morning at breakfast after she admired the brunette's system for taking notes. Rebecca thought she was organized, but Deirdre made her look like an amateur.

When the waitress had refilled their coffee cups, Deirdre gestured toward the footed glass dish that held her entree. "This breakfast salad is delicious," she said, referring to the layers of granola, yogurt, and fresh fruit. "You ought to try it."

Rebecca shook her head and broke off a piece of the dry toast that she'd ordered. Though lunch and dinner were served in the grand ballroom, the conference attendees were encouraged to order room service or eat breakfast in

the hotel's coffee shop to learn how a large hotel's services compared to their own inns.

"It seems like a crime not to eat here," Rebecca said,
"but I'm not very hungry. My stomach's been bothering
me." Though the indigestion hadn't worsened, it also
hadn't improved, and that surprised her. She had thought
that putting several states between her and Doug would
ease at least the pain in her stomach. The pain in her heart
would be more difficult to cure.

Nodding, Deirdre stirred sweetener into her coffee.
"It's normal. You miss your kids."

"I do," Rebecca agreed, "but I didn't feel like this when
I was in Hawaii." Of course, she reflected, Doug had been
there. He had kept her so busy that she hadn't had time to
be homesick.

"I've always wanted to go to Hawaii. Tell me, is it as
wonderful as I've heard?"

Rebecca nodded and described the Big Island. "It was
an incredible week. I'd recommend it to anyone who
wants a special vacation, but for me it was a lot more than
that." *It was the start of a whole new life.* "Being there
made me realize that I wanted to be an innkeeper. I had
been toying with the idea, but the Bradford . . ." *and Doug*
". . . made me realize that it was more than a whim." She
broke off another piece of toast. "What about you? Why
did you decide to open your B&B?"

"I think it's part of my DNA." When Rebecca raised
an eyebrow, Deirdre continued, "My parents wouldn't
vacation any other way than in B&B's, although having
seven children limited the number of inns that would
accept us." She swallowed the last of her breakfast par-
fait. "I have such fond memories of the times that we
spent in those inns that I decided I ought to open my
own."

"And knowing what your parents went through, trying

to find places big enough for you, you decided to cater to families with children." That was one area where the two women's inns differed. While Bluebonnet Spring was primarily for adults, Deirdre had designed Tall Oaks as a place for families.

"My friends claim it's because I don't have kids of my own and this gives me the chance to enjoy other people's children, but it's more than that. I believe families need a place to relax together."

"I agree." Rebecca pushed the plate of toast away. "I've been thinking." Perhaps if she focused on something else, she would be able to forget about her stomachache. The idea had been hovering in the back of her mind since the night before, and now that she'd heard Deirdre explain the reason for Tall Oaks being family-oriented, she knew it was worth considering. "Our inns aren't that far apart." Deirdre's B&B was near Austin, which, although it wasn't right around the corner, was within a few hours' drive of Bluebonnet Spring. "They have similar architectural styles." The two women had shared pictures along with crab chowder and sourdough bread the previous night. "We even have the same target audiences." When Deirdre started to shake her head, Rebecca held up her hand, urging patience. "Most of my guests have families, but when they come to Bluebonnet Spring, they want a getaway weekend. I'll bet they'd love to know about an inn where they could take the children."

Her eyes sparkling, Deirdre finished the thought. "And my guests would relish a place to escape from their children."

"Bingo! I was hoping you'd say that, because I thought we might want to consider cross-marketing."

There was no mistaking Deirdre's enthusiasm. "It's a great idea! You must be a marketing genius, because I never would have thought of that."

Rebecca shrugged. Even though she'd attended a marketing session the night before, the idea might not have occurred to her, if she hadn't spent so much time with Doug, marketer extraordinaire. She winced as another wave of pain washed over her.

"Are you okay?"

Of course she was okay. She was Rebecca Fleming Barton, the woman who was never ill. "It's just a touch of indigestion." Gathering her purse and the conference tote bag, she waved at Deirdre. "I'll meet you back here for lunch."

But by lunch the pain that had been a nagging irritation had become worse. "I'm going to skip lunch," Rebecca told her friend when they joined the queue that was filing into the ballroom. "I think I'd better lie down for a few minutes."

The brunette's eyes darkened with concern. "Your indigestion is worse?" She stepped out of line and led Rebecca to a corner where they could talk without shouting over the crowd.

"Much worse," Rebecca confirmed. "And now the pain is all in one spot."

A flicker of concern crossed Deirdre's face. "Your lower right abdomen?" When Rebecca nodded, Deirdre put her hand on Rebecca's forehead. This time her concern was obvious. "You're running a fever, my friend. We need to get you to the hospital pronto!"

For Rebecca, the next hour seemed like déjà vu. The ambulance, the sirens, and the bright lights of the emergency room were all familiar to her. The difference was that this time she was the patient, not the anxious mother of a critically ill boy.

She winced as the doctor poked and prodded. Though his face remained impassive, the questions he asked frightened Rebecca as much as the worsening pain. "It's appendicitis," he said. "We're going to have to operate."

Almost before she knew what was happening, the anesthesiologist was telling her she would soon feel very sleepy. Rebecca's last memory was of a pain spearing through her and a voice in the distance that sounded like hers calling out Doug's name.

When she opened her eyes, she was in a small room that seemed surprisingly homey. The starkness of the white walls was relieved by a stenciled border of entwined ivy leaves, the muted green repeated in the curtain that separated Rebecca's half of the room from the other.

"You're a lucky woman." The nurse smiled pleasantly as she checked Rebecca's vital stats. "Your friend has six younger brothers, who have—according to her—managed to spend more time in emergency rooms than any family ought to. She said that's why she recognized the symptoms." The nurse scribbled something on Rebecca's chart. "She got you here in the nick of time."

"Did my appendix burst?" That was, Rebecca knew, what the doctor had feared.

The nurse shook her head. "No, but it was close. Another hour and . . ."

There was no need to finish the sentence. Another hour without treatment and Rebecca might have died. "Is Deirdre here?"

"You didn't think I'd let them chase me away, did you?" Deirdre asked when the nurse showed her into Rebecca's room. "Some kind of friend that would be!" She studied Rebecca's face, then announced. "You're looking a lot better than you were a few hours ago."

"I feel better, even though I suspect it's the result of the meds."

"Don't argue with success." Deirdre settled into the chair next to Rebecca's bed. "I found your sister's name and cell phone number in your wallet. She'll be here tomorrow afternoon. That was the earliest flight she could get."

Deirdre, it appeared, had thought of everything. "I don't know what to say other than thank you."

"That's what friends are for. But if you want to do something, you can pay me back by bringing your family to my inn. I want to meet your kids."

Deirdre had a strange idea of payback. "That's more work for you," Rebecca told her. "A better thank you would be for you to come to Bluebonnet Spring. That way you could relax."

Deirdre shook her head. "I'll take a raincheck on that. I was thinking about next week when you're still recuperating. You could rest at Tall Oaks, and I'd have the fun of playing with your children." She shrugged. "If it works out well, you could always write a testimonial about how wonderful it is to recover from surgery at Tall Oaks. That might open up whole new markets for me."

Before Rebecca could reply, the nurse came in, telling Deirdre visiting hours were over, leaving Rebecca alone with her thoughts, thoughts that centered on the man who'd come to her inn to recuperate. She closed her eyes, remembering the day he'd arrived, when surprise had mingled with pleasure and fear. As if she were looking through a kaleidoscope, the memory changed, shifting to the day Doug had taken them all to the zoo, shifting again to the night of their blind date. And then, seemingly of their own volition, her memories jumped to the day Doug had asked her to marry him, the day she'd admitted her fears.

Rebecca's eyes flew open, and she looked around the

room. Though it was attractive, it was still a hospital room. *Her* hospital room.

What had she done? Rebecca's heart began to pound as she recognized the enormity of her actions. She had been wrong, so very, very wrong. She had refused Doug's love because she had wanted him to give her an ironclad guarantee that he wouldn't have another heart attack and that he wouldn't leave her and the children alone. Her fears had been so strong that she had asked for the impossible, knowing Doug could never give it to her. He could have lied, but he hadn't. Instead, though Rebecca knew that the admission had hurt him, Doug had told her the truth: life has no guarantees. And so she had pushed him away, rejecting the finest gift anyone could offer her, simply because she was afraid.

As she looked at the equipment that was even now monitoring her blood pressure, heartbeat, and oxygen absorption, Rebecca nodded slowly, her eyes filling with tears as she thought of the pain she had inflicted on Doug. He had been right. There were no guarantees. Though she had worried about him, Rebecca was the one who had almost died. She shuddered, thinking how close she had come to never holding her children again. Life was infinitely precious. Doug was right about that. He was also right about another thing. Rebecca had been a coward. She had been afraid to take a chance, afraid to let herself love. But that was over. Tomorrow . . . Before she could complete the thought, she drifted into sleep.

Twelve hours later Rebecca had finished her breakfast and was feeling distinctly more human after the nurse had allowed her to wash her hair and put on makeup. At least when Rachel arrived this afternoon, she would look as if she were on the road to recovery.

"You have a visitor."

Rebecca nodded, thankful that she was allowed out of bed today. She and Deirdre—for that must be who the visitor was—could sit near the window, and maybe by the time Rachel arrived, Rebecca would be able to walk to the lounge.

But the footsteps were heavier than Deirdre's, and the person who entered her room was definitely not Deirdre.

"Doug!" Rebecca's heart began to race. The man she dreamed about each night, the man who filled so many of her waking thoughts, the man she loved beyond all reason, was here. Though he looked haggard, dark circles under his eyes indicating that he hadn't slept, to Rebecca he seemed more handsome than ever. "I'm so glad to see you!" She had been afraid that he would have gone back to Detroit by now.

Rebecca held out both hands, clasping his and drawing him further into the room. "We'd better sit down," she said, pointing to the chairs. It wasn't only her illness that made her legs feel like jelly. It was the fact that Doug, whom she had thought she would never again see, was here.

He looked at the room. "I should have brought flowers."

"I'd rather look at you than flowers." Though it was nothing less than the truth, a day ago Rebecca wouldn't have admitted it. So much had changed in a few hours.

"I wasn't sure of my reception after the way we parted," Doug admitted as he drew his chair closer to hers, "but I couldn't stay away. When I heard what happened, I had to see for myself that you were all right. I convinced Rachel she should stay with Danny and Laura and let me come to San Francisco."

Rebecca chuckled. "I imagine you didn't have to twist her arm too hard. Rachel never did like flying—except for hot air balloons."

A nurse's aide popped her head into the room, then left when she saw that Rebecca had a visitor.

"Rachel did mention that," Doug admitted. A wry smile crossed his face as he continued, "I suspect that was only part of the reason she let me come in her place. When she told me about you, I was so scared that I wouldn't be surprised if Rachel was afraid I'd worry the kids."

"Do they know?"

Doug shook his head. "All Rachel told them is that you're not feeling well and will have to stay here a couple days longer. Danny said that was okay as long as you bring a new rawhide bone for Doxy and a jigsaw puzzle for him."

"A jigsaw puzzle?" Her son had never played with one.

Doug crossed his legs and leaned back in the chair. Other than his wrinkled clothing and the circles under his eyes, he did not look like a man who'd spent the night on an airplane. "Rachel was having trouble getting Danny to sleep. Bedtime stories didn't seem to work, so I hooked him on a puzzle one night, then told him we could finish it only if he was rested."

"And that worked?"

"Like a charm." Doug flashed her a grin that told her how proud he was of his ploy's success. "He may not have fallen asleep immediately, but he was so quiet, we couldn't tell."

Rebecca shook her head in wonder. "I can't believe how good you are with him." Though the man had no children, and, by his own admission, no nieces or nephews, he seemed to have an instinctive knowledge of what young children needed.

"I told you the truth, Rebecca. I love your children and wish they were mine." He swallowed deeply, then reached for her hands. "This may not be the right time or place, but—"

She couldn't let him continue. "No, Doug."

His eyes widened in surprise, and there was no mistaking the pain that filled his eyes. "Won't you even let me finish?"

"No." Rebecca shook her head again. "But not for the reason you're probably thinking." She took a deep breath. When she had made her resolution, she hadn't thought she would have to act on it so quickly. She had expected to have more time to prepare. Scarlett O'Hara was right. Tomorrow was another day. Rebecca could always wait. *No! That was the coward's way.* She mustered every ounce of courage she possessed.

"You're right," she told Doug. "This isn't the place I would have chosen, but what happened yesterday made me realize that you were right about a lot of things." She squeezed Doug's hands, drawing strength from their warmth. How wonderful it would be to always have him by her side, to be able to hold his hand each day, to see his face across the table every morning and night. "I was a coward. I didn't want to admit it, but you were right about that. I was throwing away a chance at happiness because I wanted a guarantee that it would last. You told me there were no guarantees, and you were right about that too. I heard that message loud and clear yesterday when I was being rushed through the streets of San Francisco in an ambulance."

Doug started to speak, but Rebecca shook her head. She had to finish what she'd started. It was important. Vitally important. There were words that she needed to say, that he needed to hear. "I learned a lot yesterday. One of the things I learned was that the only thing that matters is love." He might turn away. He might tell her he didn't believe in granting second chances. She would have to take the risk, because if there was one thing Rebecca knew, it was that she couldn't go through life without telling Doug how much she loved him.

"I love you, Doug," she said, her voice cracking with emotion. "I can't give you any guarantees. I can't promise that I'll live to be a hundred. All I can promise is that I'll love you every single day that we're given."

Rebecca watched a smile bloom on Doug's face as he recognized his own words. "Will you marry me, Doug? Will you help me raise Danny and Laura, and, if we're blessed, a child of our own?" She echoed his words again.

Doug rose and drew her to her feet, his smile vanquishing her last doubts. "There's nothing on earth that I want more than to marry you and raise your children . . . our children." For a moment all he did was smile. Then he pulled her into his arms and pressed a kiss on her lips. It was long and sweet and so filled with love that Rebecca wished it would never end. At last Doug wrenched his lips from hers. "I love you, Rebecca. I always will."

She leaned back in the circle of his arms and looked up at the face she loved so dearly. "I love you more than I ever dreamed it was possible to love a man. You're everything I ever wanted." Rebecca smiled again. "I think I knew that the first time I saw you."

Doug started humming "Stranger in Paradise." "What do you think about a honeymoon in Hawaii?" he asked. "A real one this time."

Her heart filled with joy, Rebecca grinned. "That would be perfect—just like you!"

Epilogue

One month later.

"It's not fair, Mom." Danny squirmed as Rebecca knotted his tie. This was the last thing she had to do before she put on her own dress and the circlet of bluebonnets that she was wearing as a headpiece.

"What's the matter, honey? I thought you wanted to be my ring bearer the way you were for Aunt Rachel." When he had heard that Rebecca and Doug were going to get married, Danny had been overjoyed. He'd raced around the inn, telling everyone who would listen that he was getting a new dad and that he was going to have the very important job of carrying wedding rings. Now, it appeared, he was having second thoughts.

"That's okay," he said, squirming again when Rebecca brushed his hair one last time.

"Then what's wrong?"

"It's Doxy," he said, a plaintive tone to his voice. "It's not fair that she can't come."

"Danny, Doxy's a dog."

"But, Mom . . ." The mulish expression on her son's face

told Rebecca he was preparing to sulk. "Doxy's part of the family. Doug said so."

And so it was that as Rebecca walked down the garden path toward the gazebo where Bluebonnet Spring's first wedding would occur, she was preceded by her matron of honor, her ring bearer, and a brown dachshund.

Author's Letter

Dear Reader,

It's always with regret that I type the words "the end." Even though I'm happy that another book is finished and will soon be ready for you to read, there's a sadness about saying good-bye to the characters. During the course of plotting and writing, they've become my friends, and it's never easy to say farewell to friends. That's why I started giving some of my favorite characters parts in other books.

I had a lot of fun bringing the heroes and heroines of earlier books into *Bluebonnet Spring*. If you were intrigued by the hints I dropped about Rachel's marriage, *Strings Attached* will answer them. Luke, who's trying to prove that he's the best parent, didn't have an easy time, as you'll discover in *Imperfect Together*, and Judith Hibbard, the author who helped promote Bluebonnet Spring, has her own story in *Moonlight Masquerade*.

Then there's Deirdre. No, I haven't written her story yet, but when she appeared at the innkeepers' conference, I knew she was going to be the heroine of my next *Unwanted Legacy* romance. Deirdre's impatient, so I'd better start plotting her story. In the meantime, if you enjoy historical romances, I hope you'll look for my *War Brides Trilogy*. Set during World War I, *Dancing in the Rain, Whistling in the Dark*, and *Laughing at the Thunder* are the stories of three sisters from—where else?— Canela who are caught up in the War to End All Wars and who learn that love and adventure can be found in even the most unlikely places.

Happy reading!

Amanda Harte